MORE TALES FROM GRIMM

MORE TALES
FROM GRIMM

FREELY TRANSLATED
AND ILLUSTRATED BY
WANDA GÁG

COWARD, McCANN & GEOGHEGAN, INC.

NEW YORK

First paperback edition 1981
Printed in the United States of America
LCC 81-66879   ISBN 0-698-20534-0

FOREWORD

This is Wanda Gág's last book. She was working on and had substantially completed More Tales from Grimm *when she succumbed to a fatal illness in June of 1946. The translation of the text had reached the stage of final revision, and thus was ready for the press. The illustrations presented a slightly more difficult problem. There were on hand almost a hundred usable drawings. Of these about three quarters were in their final pen-and-ink form, finished for reproduction as line blocks. The balance were in varying stages of completeness, yet sufficiently realized to be passable as illustrations. As usual, Wanda Gág had sketched out a rough dummy for the layout of the text and pictures. It seemed, in the judgment of her literary and artistic executors, Earle Humphreys and myself, that the whole work was so nearly complete that it could go out into the world without in any way compromising her reputation as a writer or artist. Publication was therefore authorized; and the book was carried through to press by her husband, Earle Humphreys, her sister, Flavia Gág, and the publisher's editor, Rose Dobbs, all of whom had a sympathetic understanding of the author's point of view.*

More Tales from Grimm, *by reason of these circumstances, will give the public—more than customarily happens—a glimpse behind the scenes, as it were, a fuller realization of the painstaking labor that is expended before a book is actually printed. Just as the author may polish and revise the text until it achieves the desired perfection of style and phrasing, so the illustrator may do over a drawing several times before he is satisfied that it fully expresses the pictorial idea. A few examples of the preliminary stages for illustration are perforce included in this book; and they reveal Wanda Gág's characteristic method of developing a theme. As she worked on the translation of the text, she would jot down an idea for an appropriate illustration. This might merely be a scribble of essential lines, a kind of artist's shorthand. Numerous such drawings exist for this work, including some delightful ones which she never had opportunity to develop; but unfortunately they could not be reproduced because they were too summary in execution. In the next step she would expand the first thought into a somewhat more complete drawing in pencil or in ink. Characteristic examples of this type are the pictures for* The Earth Gnome *and* The Wolf and the Seven Little Kids, *or, in an even more primitive stage, in pencil, the duckling drawing the cart as on page 77 or* The Rabbit and the Hedgehog *on page 168. All of these preliminary drawings are fully realized as illustrations— the dramatic action and character are all there—the pictures merely have not been translated into the style best adapted for reproduction as line blocks. They more than make up in spontaneity and verve what they lack in finish. Mention should be made of the drawing for* The Soldier and His Magic Helpers *on page 63, because it reveals how Wanda Gág, in spite of her capacity for meticulous detail, slipped up on a minor point. In the text the Blower always functions through his nostril, whereas in her preliminary sketch he is definitely shown blowing through his mouth. Undoubtedly had she lived, the artist would have noticed the discrepancy and corrected it in the final drawing. It will be interesting to discover how many readers are sharp-eyed enough to discover the lapse. Incidentally all the drawings in the book are faithfully reproduced without any retouch or correction by a foreign hand. Fortunately the great bulk of the illustrations had already been done over in her finished style, ready for the engraver. If she had been granted more time, she would certainly have increased the number of illustrations by developing certain sketches that are roughly suggested in the dummy. Yet the work is substantially complete; and it is fortunate that at least one illustration exists for every story in the book.*

Wanda Gág was particularly qualified to translate and illustrate Grimm's Tales. She was born in Minnesota of pioneer Bohemian stock, and grew up in the German-speaking community of New Ulm. She was nourished on the old-world tales of Grimm, Bechstein, and Andersen. Her peasant heritage made her receptive to the homely wisdom and common sense which permeates Grimm's stories; and her child's sense of wonder—which she never lost—made her sympathetic to the uncommon sense and fairytale elements contained in them. These qualities, combined with her dramatic instinct for story-telling, made her a perfect interpreter of Grimm, and I was delighted when the complete German edition of The Tales, which I gave her in 1931, bore such beauti-ful fruit in words and pictures. Important, too, was the fact that, as both author and illustrator, she could achieve a compelling unity of effect in a work such as Grimm's, which somehow seems to call for pictorial embellish-ment. Her work thus belongs in that rare but ideal cate-gory of the illustrated book where the writer and artist are one.

CARL ZIGROSSER

To
Barbara Jean
Lydia Mary and Sara
Pat and Janey
Jeanne and Johnny
Rus and Anne
Eric
Judy

THE GOLDEN KEY

ONCE upon a time—it was winter and a deep blanket of snow lay over the ground—a poor boy went forth with his sledge to gather some wood in the forest. He became very cold, and after he had gathered a load of wood and piled it high on his sledge, he began scraping away the snow so that he might build a fire at which to warm himself. And what do you think?—while he was doing so, he found a tiny golden key buried beneath the snow!

"Where there is a key, there might also be a lock," thought the boy, and, after digging more deeply in the ground, he found an iron chest.

"Now if the key will only fit!" he said. "I'm sure there must be wonderful treasures in that chest."

He looked and looked for a keyhole but could not find any. At last he found it—a very tiny one—and when he tried the key, behold!—it fitted exactly. He turned the key once around, and—

...now we must wait until the boy has unlocked it completely and has opened the lid—then we shall find out what treasures and wonders are in that chest!

TABLE OF CONTENTS

CONTENTS

LIST OF FULL PAGE ILLUSTRATIONS

THE SEVEN SWABIANS

ONCE upon a time there were seven Swabians who put their heads together and decided to go out to see the world. As they hoped to meet with great adventures and to perform many a mighty deed, they considered it best to be well armed.

"What kind of weapons would be best for us?" they wondered, and at last, thinking it safest to stay close together, they decided on a single weapon to be used by all. So they had it made—one long, strong spear—after which they stood up beside it in a row, every man in his place and ready for action.

1

Master Schulz was the first and bravest.

Yockli was the second.

Marli was the third.

Yergli was the fourth.

Michal was the fifth.

Hansi was the sixth.

Veitli was the least and last.

Each grasped the spear with his strong right hand, and then away they went, full of fire and hope. For days they marched, and for many a weary mile, but wherever they went all was peaceful and quiet. No dragons, no foes, no robbers, no thieves, no wild and furious beasts came their way. Alas! Was there no adventure left in the world?

At last something happened!

It was a hot afternoon in the hay month, and our seven brave warriors were trudging through a large meadow more asleep than awake. Toward the end of the day as twilight was falling they came to a thicket, and as they passed it, out flew a great big hornet. It was buzzing crossly. In the dim light the seven braves could not see what it was, and when they heard its loud

Brr-um! Brr-um!
Brr-um, bum, bum!

2

they shrank together in terror. As for Master Schulz, he was so frightened that he broke out in a cold sweat and almost let go of the spear. "Hark! Hark! I hear a drum!" he cried. "Oh Heavens, what shall we do?"

And Yockli cried, "It must be the foe, and it's near-by too, for I can smell the powder!"

At these words Master Schulz dropped his end of the spear and began to run. As he leaped over a hedge to make his escape, he tripped on a rake which had been left there by the haymakers. The rake sprang up and hit him in the face and he, thinking it was the foe, yelled:

> Capture me! Capture me!
> I give myself up!

When the others heard the words of their mighty leader, they followed him, tumbling over the hedge one after the other, and shouting:

> If you give up, so do we!
> If you give up, so do we!

Then they all waited, hardly daring to breathe and prepared for the worst. Nothing happened. By-and-by they picked themselves up, brushed the ground and grass from their clothes, and looked around. No one was there. They

3

looked at each other without a word and at last Master
Schulz spoke up.

"My men," he said, "my warriors brave and true, this
was a perilous adventure to be sure. But I think," here he
lowered his voice, "I think we had best not tell about it
at home."

The others agreed, bobbing their heads; then once more
all seven picked up the long, strong spear, stood in a sturdy
straight line, and with a "Left, right, left!" they traveled
on. For days they marched, feeling full of valor and ready
for any fray, and at last adventure crossed their path once
more—yes, an adventure indeed, one which made their first
one seem like nothing!

As before, it happened late in the day. The way of our
doughty braves took them through a fallow field where
they spied something among the furrows—a creature lying
asleep with its ears standing up and its glassy eyes wide
open! The seven, hardly daring to look at the beast, peeped
fearfully at it out of the corners of their eyes and tried to
decide upon the least dangerous course of action.

"Shall we catch it?" asked Yergli.

"It looks fierce," said Yockli.

"Wild too," said Marli.

"And none too small," said Michal.

"Its ears are over-long," said Hansi.

"Its whiskers too," piped Veitli.

"Let's flee!" cried several.

"But if we flee," said Master Schulz, "the thing might follow us and swallow us up. No, no!" he shouted. "This dangerous beast must be vanquished, and we—we must be stout of heart and steady of hand. To battle, my braves!"

Now each man in his place grasped the spear and bent forward as though getting ready to charge, but aside from that nothing happened. Master Schulz was always trying to keep the spear back, but little Veitli, who stood at the very end and was farthest from the monster, wanted to dash forward, and cried:

> Strike home, in every Swabian's name!
> Shall we be cowards to our shame?

But Hansi said to him:

> You've easy talking way back there.
> You're safe enough—why should you care?

Then Michal yelled:

> Oh hulla, hui! Come, let's run!
> I'm sure it is the Evil one!

And Yergli said:

> And if not he, then 'tis his mother
> Or else his father or stepbrother.

Then Yockli said:

> Our Schulz is valiant, that we know
> He'll surely rout the fearsome foe.

At this Master Schulz gathered up his courage and said solemnly:

> Advance, my men! Each do his share.
> Brave folk like we must do and dare!

At that all seven lunged forward and with blazing eyes charged upon the monster. Master Schulz crossed himself and prayed for help from Heaven, but as he found himself getting closer and closer to the enemy, he became so frightened that he screamed, "Hie, hie! Ho, ho! Hee, hee!" in the greatest anguish.

At this bloodcurdling sound the monster awoke, gave a startled look, and hopped swiftly away. As for Master Schulz, when he saw that the foe was fleeing, he found courage at last to take a good look at it. What he saw made him cry joyfully:

> Ho, fellow heroes, ho, look there!
> The monster's nothing but a hare!

And so the seven warriors wandered on, well pleased with themselves. No doubt they had other exciting and perilous adventures, but as they never told anyone about them, no one told me—and so, of course, I can't tell you.

THE WOLF AND THE FOX

THERE was once a greedy wolf who had a fox living with him, and because the fox was the weaker of the two, he always had to do whatever the wolf wanted him to. The fox liked this little enough and would have gladly been rid of his master.

Now it happened that once, as the two were going through the forest, the wolf said, "Red Fox, find me something to eat or I will gobble you up instead."

To which the fox replied, "Well, I know of a farmyard in which there are two little lambs. If you like, we'll go there and I'll fetch one of them for your supper tonight."

That suited the wolf, and they went to the farmyard where the fox deftly stole one of the lambs, gave it to the wolf, and went on his way. But the wolf, after he had eaten the lamb, didn't feel full and, greedy as he was, wanted the second lamb as well.

"I can easily get it myself, now that I know where to go," he thought; and off he went to do so. But because he was so clumsy about it, the mother sheep heard him coming and began to bleat and cry so fearfully that the peasants came running out to see what was the matter. They found the wolf and beat him so unmercifully that he ran limping and howling back to his home in the forest.

"You certainly misled me that time," said the wolf to the fox. "It was you who thought of getting the lamb, and when I went to get the other one, the peasants surprised me and beat me to a pulp."

The fox merely said, "Why are you such a glutton?"

The next day as they went out into the field, the wolf said again, "Red Fox, find me something to eat or I'll gobble you up instead." To which the fox replied, "I know of a farmhouse where tonight the woman is frying pancakes. If you like, we'll go there and fetch some of them for your supper."

They went there and the fox, very clever about it as usual, sneaked around the house, and peered and sniffed

10

about until he discovered where the plate of pancakes stood. Then he deftly pulled down six pancakes and brought them to the wolf.

"There, now you have something to stuff yourself with," said the fox and went his way.

In the twinkling of an eye the wolf gulped down the six pancakes, then said to himself, "They taste like more, and I'll get them, too!"

He hurried to the farmhouse and found the pancakes, but in his awkwardness he pulled down the whole platter so that it broke into pieces with a loud crash and clatter. The noise brought the farmwife, who called the menfolk, who gave the wolf such a beating that he ran to the fox in the forest, lamed in two legs and howling terribly.

"Again you gave me a bad lead!" the wolf cried angrily. "The peasants caught and lamed me, and tanned my hide for me to boot."

But the fox merely said, "Why are you such a glutton?"

On the third day when they went out together the wolf, still limping painfully, said again, "Red Fox, find me something to eat or I'll gobble you up instead."

To which the fox answered, "Very well. I know a man

who has a tub full of freshly salted meat in his cellar. We'll fetch a bit of that for ourselves."

"Good," said the wolf. "But I am still lame and I don't want to get beaten up again, so this time I'll go all the way with you right at the start so that you can help me in case I get into trouble."

"As you will," said the fox, and showed him many little twists and turns and secret paths by which at length they found their way to the cellar. Ah! Here was meat in abundance, and the wolf, without wasting a minute, set to work at it, thinking, "This is good, and it will be a long time before I stop!"

The fox, too, enjoyed himself mightily at this delectable meal; but he stopped often to look about him, and ran occasionally to the hole by which they had come in, to find out if he was still thin enough to slip through it.

Seeing this, the wolf said, "Dear Fox, do tell me— why must you always be going back and forth so much, jumping out and then in again?"

"Oh," said the sly fox, "I must look often to find out whether anyone is coming. But I must warn you, don't eat too much!"

"As to that," said the wolf, "I am not going to leave this place until the tub is empty."

He ate and ate, and as he gulped and gobbled away, the fox darted back and forth until at last the farmer, hearing the noise of the fox's jumping, came down into the cellar to see what was going on there.

As soon as the fox saw him he leaped out through the hole at one bound. The wolf tried to follow him but he had eaten himself so fat that he stuck fast in the hole and couldn't get through. Then the farmer came and beat the wolf until he fell dead, but the fox bounded off into the forest and was mightily glad that he was rid of the greedy glutton at last.

MOTHER HOLLE

THERE was once a widow who had two daughters. Both were called Marie, but one of them was lazy and homely while the other was pretty and industrious. Yet the widow favored the lazy girl, who was her own daughter, and she hated the industrious one who was her stepdaughter. Really, she could not bear the sight of the pretty child and so, while the lazy one lolled around and did nothing, the stepdaughter was shoved out into the kitchen to work, or sent outdoors to a well near the highway where she was made to spin until her fingers bled.

One day as the stepchild was sitting beside the well, spinning as usual, her shuttle slipped from her hand into the water and, because she was afraid of being scolded for losing the shuttle, she sprang into the well to look for it. But it was not a well like any other, for, although the poor girl fainted, she did not drown; and when she recovered from her swoon, she was not in the water at all, but in a beautiful meadow which was bright with sunshine and gay with a thousand flowers.

As she wandered along a little path which wound through this flower-dotted meadow, she came to an oven filled with bread; and right away, too, the bread began to talk.

"Oh, take me out," said the bread. "Please take me out or I'll surely get scorched. I'm baked to a turn already." This the girl was glad to do, and after drawing out the brown and fragrant loaves with the bread-shovel, she wandered on.

Next she came to a tree so thickly hung with apples that it was a wonder to see. And the apples cried out to her, "Oh, shake us, shake us, please! We're red and ripe, and ready to be gathered."

The girl shook the tree gladly enough; shook it and

16

shook it until the fruit fell around her like rain. When no more apples were left on the tree, she gathered them into a large heap on the ground and wandered on.

At last she came to a little hut from which peered an old woman with oh! such long, big teeth that the girl was frightened and wanted to run away. But the woman said, "What are you afraid of, dear child? I am Mother Holle. I will do you no harm; indeed, if you should care to stay with me and keep my house clean and neat, everything shall go well with you. But one thing I must warn you about. When you make up my bed you must shake my featherbed thoroughly—shake it and shake it until the feathers flutter about, for that is what makes the snow fall on the earth."

After hearing the old woman speak in such a friendly

manner, the girl was no longer afraid and agreed to stay. She did her work with a will, and every day she took up Mother Holle's featherbed and shook it so vigorously that the feathers fluttered about and fell as a flurry of snowflakes on the earth. In return for her good work she was treated well, had boiled or roast meat every day, and never, never heard an angry word. And yet in time she became sad. At first she could not tell what was the matter with her, but at last she knew that she was homesick for the earth; and although she was many times better off with Mother Holle than at home, still she had a longing to be there.

When she told Mother Holle about it, the old woman said, "That is good and right. I have no wish to keep you here against your will, and because you have been so obedient and have done your work so well, I myself will show you the way back."

With this, she took the girl's hand and led her to a large door which opened as they neared it.

"Stand in this doorway," said Mother Holle, and as the girl did so, a shower of golden rain fell down upon her, and clung to her head and shoulders and dress and shoes, so that she was fairly covered with it.

18

"That is your reward for being such a good girl," said Mother Holle, "and here is your shuttle, too, the one which fell into the well."

Then the great door closed, Mother Holle was gone, and the girl found herself once more on the earth, standing beside the well not far from her mother's house. And as she went into the yard, a rooster sitting on the well crowed out:

> Keekeri, keekeri, kee!
> Here comes our Gold Marie.

When the stepmother and her lazy daughter spied the girl so richly bedecked with gold, they greeted her with open arms. And when the mother heard the girl's wonderful tale, she was determined to have her own daughter try her luck in the same way.

So the lazy girl set out to do everything just as her stepsister had done. She sat at the well with a spinning wheel, dropped the shuttle into the water, and plunged in after it; and soon she, like her sister, found herself walking along the little path in the sunny, flowery meadow. Yes, and she came to the oven, too; but when she heard the bread begging to be taken out, she said

19

haughtily, "Oh indeed! And get myself all black?" And when she came to the apple tree it was the same, for when the apples asked to be taken down, she cried, "Oh indeed! And perhaps get struck on the head by one of you big apples?"

When at last she stood before the hut of Mother Holle she was not afraid, for of course she had already heard of those big, long teeth. Boldly she walked up to the door and right away, too, she asked to be taken into the old woman's service. Mother Holle said she could stay and told her what to do.

Well, on the first day the girl was most obedient and worked hard, but not because she wanted to be helpful. Oh no, she did it only for the gold which was to be poured over her. On the second day she worked much less, and on the third morning she could hardly be got out of bed. As for the important task of making it snow on earth by shaking up the old woman's featherbed, the girl did it so poorly that on the fourth day Mother Holle told her that her service was at an end and that she could now go home. This was just what the girl had been waiting for, and to herself she said, "Now it is time for the rain of gold!" Joyfully she followed Mother

Holle to the big door, but as she was standing beneath it, instead of the shower of gold, a big kettleful of sticky pitch was emptied over her.

"That is the reward for your service," said Mother Holle, and shut the door.

So the lazy girl came home, · not shimmering with precious gold, but covered with black, sticky pitch. And

as she went into the yard the rooster sitting on the well crowed out:

> Keekeri, keekeri, kee!
> Here comes our Pitch Marie.

The pitch stuck fast to her, clung to her head and shoulders and clothes, and never, as long as she lived, could she get it off.

THE WATER NIXIE

BROTHERKIN and Sisterkin were playing beside a fountain, when—plump!—they both fell in. Down below lived a Water Nixie, and when she saw the children, she said, "Now that I have you here, you shall work hard for me," and with that she carried them off with her.

Well, from then on, things went none too well for the children. Brotherkin was made to cut down a tree with a blunt ax, Sisterkin was forced to carry water in a bottomless bucket and to spin with dirty, tangled flax; and for their meals they never had anything to eat but dumplings as heavy and hard as stones.

Brotherkin and Sisterkin soon became weary of this life, so one Sunday after the Nixie had gone to church they ran away. But when church was over and the Nixie saw that her two little birds had flown, she hurried after them with leaps and bounds.

The children saw her from afar, but Sisterkin took something out of her pocket and tossed it behind her. It was a hairbrush which grew and grew until it became a big brush-hill covered with thousands and thousands of bristles.

But do you think that stopped the Nixie? Oh no! She scrambled over the bristly brush-hill and wildly ran after the children once more.

At that Brotherkin took something out of his pocket and tossed it behind him. It was a comb which grew and grew until it became a mountain of combs with thousands of teeth sticking up.

But this didn't stop the Water Nixie either. Quite nimbly she climbed and clung to the teeth, clambered over them, and ran after the children once more.

Now Sisterkin tossed behind her a looking-glass which

grew and grew until it became a hill of mirrors—a hill so smooth and slippery that the Nixie couldn't possibly get over it.

Still she wouldn't give up!

"I'll hurry home," she thought, "and fetch my ax so that I can cut a path through that glassy, glittery hill of mirrors," and she did it, too. But by the time she had returned and cut her way through the glass, the children had escaped, and the Water Nixie had to trot back to her fountain home and get her work done as best she could.

THE MOUSE, THE BIRD,
AND THE SAUSAGE

ONCE there was a tiny cottage and in it lived no
people, only a mouse, a bird, and a sausage. There they
had kept house most joyously together for many years,
and had even been able to save some money besides.

Each of the three had a daily task to do, and this is
what they did: the bird flew out into the woods and
gathered sticks with which to make the fire; the mouse
fetched water from the brook, lit the fire and set the
table; and the big, fat, jolly sausage cooked the meals.

In this way the three companions had been happy for

a long time, and might be so still, if the bird had only been contented with her lot. But very often those who are already well off, foolishly wish for something better, and that was the case with our little bird.

One day she met another bird, and as they were talking about this and that, the little bird said, "The mouse and the sausage and I—oh, we live together so happily, have all we need and more. And we each do our share of the work, that's what makes it so peaceful."

But the other bird said, "Oh, you poor ninny—you certainly are letting your two friends make a fool of you! Here you have to fly about in the woods and carry heavy loads all the time while they stay snugly at home, enjoying a life of ease."

The little bird thought this over for a while and then she said, "Yes, the mouse does have an easy time of it. All she has to do is to fetch some water and build a fire, and then she can go to her room and rest until it's time to set the table. As for the sausage, all he has to do is to watch the food and see that it is cooking well; and then, when it is time for dinner, get into the pot and swish himself around a little in the soup or vege-tables, so as to salt or flavor them."

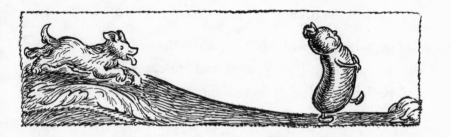

"See, what did I tell you?" said the other bird and flew away.

The next morning, with such thoughts whirling around in her little head, the bird refused to go out to the woods.

"I've been your slave long enough," she told the mouse and the sausage, "and you can't make a fool of me any longer. It's time we made a change so that I'll have an easy time of it too, for once."

The mouse and the sausage were afraid that a new arrangement might not work out so well, but in spite of all they could say, the bird insisted on having her own way, and so at last they drew lots to settle the matter. Well, it came out that the sausage, who was almost too fat to walk, was to go out and gather the wood; and the mouse, who knew nothing of cooking, was to make the meals; while the bird was to fetch the water, light the fire and set the table.

Now just look what happened!

The sausage went off to gather the wood, but so good did he smell and so plump and juicy did he look, that before long a dog followed him and ate him up.

The mouse, in the meantime, had begun cooking the dinner; but when she finally got into the pot, as the sausage used to do, to stir and flavor the soup, she was scalded and so lost her life.

Now, when the bird came in to set the table, no cook was there. In vain she called and searched, and tossed the wood here and there, hoping to find the missing mouse. In this way some of the wood caught fire and the flames began to spread. Quickly the bird ran for some water, but the bucket fell into the well and she after it, and that was the end of her too.

Now wouldn't it have been better if the bird had left things as they were, with everybody doing the work which was best suited to them?

THORN ROSE,
THE SLEEPING BEAUTY

ONCE upon a time—oh, that was many years ago—
there lived a King and Queen who said every day, "Alas,
if we only had a child!" But year after year passed by
and still their wish was not granted.

Now it happened that one day as the Queen was
bathing in a pool, a frog crawled out of the water and
said to her, "Your wish will soon be granted. Before
the year is up a daughter shall be born to you."

And what the frog promised came true. Within the
year a daughter was born, a child so wondrously beautiful that the King could hardly contain himself for joy.
In honor of the event he gave a great banquet to which
he invited all his friends and relatives; and, in order
that the child might be given great gifts and be protected
from harm, he also invited the Wise Women. There
were thirteen of these in his kingdom, but as he had

31

only a dozen golden plates for them to eat out of, only twelve could be invited, while the thirteenth had to stay at home.

The feast was celebrated with great pomp and splendor, and as it drew to an end, the Wise Women bestowed their wonderful gifts upon the baby Princess. One gave her virtue, another beauty, a third riches, and so on until the child had been given everything one could wish for in the world. When eleven of them had had their say, in came the uninvited thirteenth! She was very angry at not having been asked and, without greeting anybody and looking neither to right nor to left, she cried out in a loud voice, "In her fifteenth year the Princess shall prick her finger with a spindle and fall lifeless to the floor!" Then without another word she turned her back upon them and left the hall.

Everyone was shocked, and a dead silence fell upon the company; but now the twelfth Wise Woman, whose gift had not yet been bestowed, stepped forward.

"The curse of our uninvited sister has been spoken," she said, "but while I cannot undo it, yet I have the power to soften it. So this is my gift to the Princess: although she will fall lifeless to the floor, it shall not be

32

death but only a hundred years' sleep which shall overtake her."

However, the King, wishing to save his child from even this misfortune, issued a decree that every spinning wheel in his kingdom should be burned.

.   .   .   .   .

All the wishes of the twelve Wise Women came true. The Princess grew up so beautiful, charming and clever, and so kind and modest besides, that none who saw her could help loving her.

So time went on until the fifteen years had passed. But it happened that on the very day when the Princess was fifteen years old, the King and Queen were not able to be at home, and the young girl, left to herself, decided to amuse herself by exploring the castle. Upstairs and down she wandered, peeping into the halls and bedchambers and closets as the fancy took her, until at

last she came to an old tower near the top of the castle
which she had never seen before. Here a narrow winding
stairway led to a door with a rusty key sticking in its
lock. She turned the key, and as she did so, the door
sprang open; and there in a tiny attic room sat an old
woman with a spindle, busily spinning flax.

"Good day, little old mother," said the Princess.
"What is it you are doing there?"

"I am spinning," said the woman, nodding her head
as she worked.

"But what is spinning, and what is that thing which
whirls around so merrily?" asked the Princess, for, of
course, since all the spinning wheels in the kingdom had

been ordered burned, she had never seen one before. "Let me try it too," she went on, taking the spindle in her hand to see if she also could make it whirl.

But as soon as she touched it, the curse of the thirteenth Wise Woman went into effect. The spindle pricked the Princess's finger, and in the next moment the beautiful young girl fell back upon a bed which stood there, and lay motionless in a deep, deep sleep.

And this sleep spread over the whole castle.

The King and the Queen, who had just returned, fell asleep beside their thrones, and with them the whole court and all that belonged to it.

Outside, the horses in the stables, the dappled hunting dogs in the courtyard, the ducks and the geese in the barnyard, all fell asleep just as they stood or walked or lay. On the roof the doves tucked their little heads under their wings and slept, and in the castle the flies on the walls—yes, even the fire flaring and flickering on the hearth—became dead and still, and slept like all the rest. The meat stopped roasting on the spit, and the cook, who was about to box the scullery boy's ears for some mistake he had made, let him go and went to sleep. The scullery boy, with his arm upraised to shield himself

35

from the blow, slept too; and the kitchen maid with a black fowl on her lap slumbered with her hands still among its feathers in the act of plucking it.

Outdoors in the castle-yard the wind ceased blowing, in the gardens the flowers drowsily closed their petals, and on the trees every leaf hung motionless and never moved more.

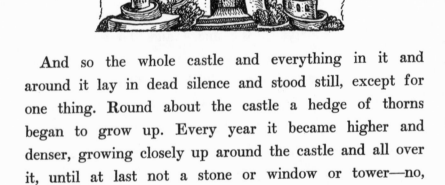

And so the whole castle and everything in it and around it lay in dead silence and stood still, except for one thing. Round about the castle a hedge of thorns began to grow up. Every year it became higher and denser, growing closely up around the castle and all over it, until at last not a stone or window or tower—no, not even the topmost banner on the roof—could be seen.

And so the years passed by, but the story of the beautiful Thorn Rose, as the Princess was called, spread over

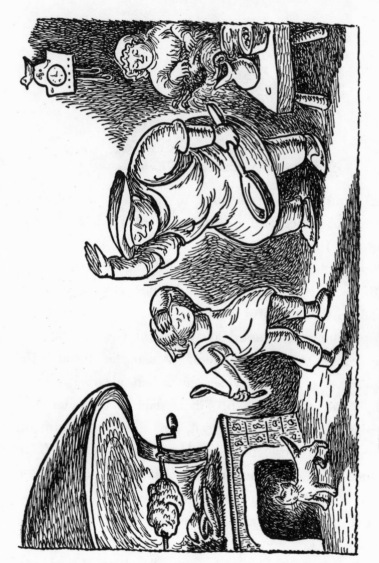

THE COOK WAS ABOUT TO BOX THE SCULLERY BOY'S EARS

all the countryside. From time to time various brave or venturesome princes came and tried to force their way through the thorny hedge to the castle. But the brambles, like thorny fingers, closed around the poor youths and held them fast so that they could not get loose again and had to die a pitiful death.

Many more years passed away and at length a foreign Prince came to the kingdom. When he beheld the strange mass of thorny vines, he asked about it.

"Ah," said an old man, "it is said that under this thicket is a castle, and in it, in deep enchantment, slumbers Thorn Rose, the Sleeping Beauty. Also a King and Queen and many others who have slept there these hundred years."

"But has no one tried to rescue them?" asked the Prince.

"Yes," answered the old man. "I have heard my

grandfather say that many a king's son has tried to get through the hedge of thorns, but none has ever succeeded."

"I will try it," said the Prince.

"No! No!" cried the old man. "I beg of you, do not waste your young life in this way."

But the Prince would not listen to him. "I have no fear," said he, "and I have a great desire to look upon this sleeping beauty, this Thorn Rose as you call her." And he set off toward the vine-covered castle.

But just think! It was now exactly a hundred years to the day since the young Princess had pricked her finger. As the Prince neared the thorn hedge it burst suddenly into bloom, becoming a mass of large, beautiful flowers which parted and bent aside of their own accord so that he could pass through unharmed, after which they again closed behind him as a thick hedge.

As for the Prince, he lost no time looking about him, and the more he saw the more his wonder grew. Everyone and everything was still fast asleep—the horses and the dappled dogs in the barnyard, the doves on the roof and the flies on the walls, the fire and the cook in the kitchen, the scullery boy who was still shielding himself from the blow which in a hundred years had never come, and the kitchen maid who had never finished plucking the black fowl in her lap. Yes, wherever he looked he saw people lying or sitting or standing in motionless slumber, servants and lords and ladies and, leaning against their thrones, the King and the Queen themselves.

But the one he was looking for he could not find.

So he went on searching, and all was so quiet that he could hear himself breathe. At last he came to the old tower near the top of the castle, and when he turned the key in the lock, the door sprang open. There, in the midst of the blossoming vines which had crept in through the window, lay the slumbering Thorn Rose, looking so beautiful that the Prince could not take his eyes from her. He looked and looked, and then bent over and kissed the fair face. In that moment Thorn Rose opened her eyes and smiled sweetly at the charming youth. How happy they both were!—the Princess because she had been released from her hundred years' sleep, and the Prince because he had at last found what he was looking for. Together they made their way down the narrow winding staircase and all through the castle; and wherever they went, there was life and movement once more.

40

The King and the Queen and all the court awoke and gazed at each other in astonishment. Outside, the horses in the stables stood up and shook themselves; the dappled hunting dogs barked and wagged their tails; the ducks and geese and chickens squawked and quacked and cackled as they began looking around for food; the doves on the roof drew their heads from under their wings, cooed happily and began flying about. The fire on the hearth flared up and crackled and went on cooking the dinner where it had left off a hundred years before; the meat on the spit began turning and sputtering; the cook gave the scullery boy the long-delayed box on the ears; and the kitchen maid began briskly plucking the fowl in her lap.

Everything was full of activity; every one was happy to be alive again. As for the Prince and Thorn Rose, they had fallen in love with each other immediately, and it was not long before they celebrated their wedding amidst gaiety and splendor.

THE SWEET PORRIDGE

ONCE there was a poor but worthy girl who lived with her mother in a little village. They were so poor, these two, that many a night they had to go hungry to bed, and at last there came a time when there was nothing left in the house for them to eat. Now the girl, hoping perhaps to find some nuts or berries, went out into the woods where she met an old woman. Strangely enough, the woman already knew that the two were in trouble and, handing the girl a little cooking kettle, she said, "Take this, my child. If you set it on the stove and say to it, 'Cook, little kettle, cook,' then it will start bubbling and boiling and will cook up a mess of good, sweet millet porridge for you and your mother.

Then, when you have eaten your fill, you need only to say, 'Stop, little kettle, stop,' and it will stop cooking until the next time."

And that was the way it turned out to be. The girl took the kettle home to her mother, and now the two

could eat all the sweet porridge they wanted and were never hungry any more.

One day the girl went away for a few hours and the mother, feeling hungry, said, "Cook, little kettle, cook." Immediately a good hearty smell filled the kitchen, the kettle began to cook, and soon the mother was enjoying a big bowlful of good, sweet porridge. But when she had eaten her fill and wanted to make the kettle stop

cooking, she found she had forgotten the right words.

So the little kettle kept on cooking—cooked and cooked until the porridge rose over the rim of the kettle. Cooked and cooked some more until it flowed all over the stove. Cooked and cooked and kept on cooking until the little cottage was filled with porridge. Cooked and cooked until it poured out of the windows into the street, and then into all the huts and cottages along the way.

At this the people ran from their houses to escape from the bubbling, boiling flood, but the porridge cooked merrily on until it had filled the whole village. Even then it didn't stop but spread out over the fields, flowing in all directions as though it were trying to feed the whole world. Everyone was worried, but no one knew what to do.

At last, when only one little hut was left unfilled with porridge, the girl returned. When she saw what had happened, she quickly cried, "Stop, little kettle, stop!" And of course the kettle obeyed and stopped cooking— but the only way the village folk could return to their houses was to eat their way through the porridge!

THE LITTLE SHEPHERD BOY

THERE was once a shepherd boy who was famed far and wide for the clever answers he gave to all the questions which were put to him. The King of the country, too, had heard tales of the boy's wisdom and, finding them hard to believe, sent for him so that he might find out the truth for himself.

When the boy arrived at the palace, the King said to him, "If you can answer wisely the three questions I am about to ask you, I will look upon you as my own son and you shall dwell here with me in my royal palace."

"And what are these questions?" asked the boy.

The King said, "The first is: how many drops of water are there in the sea?"

"Lord King," said the boy, "if you will have all the rivers in the world dammed up so that not a drop can run away before I have counted it, then I will tell you how many drops of water there are in the sea."

Since it was impossible for the King to accomplish this, he had to accept the boy's answer. Then he said, "The next question is: how many stars are there in the sky?"

The boy asked for a pen and a large sheet of paper. With the pen he made so many tiny dots on the paper that it dazzled one's eyes to look at them; and as for counting them, no one could have done it. Then, handing the paper to the King, he said, "There are as many stars in the sky as there are dots on this paper. Just count them and see."

But as no one was able to do so, the King had to accept the boy's answer. Then he said, "The third question is: how many seconds of time are there in eternity?"

To this the boy replied, "In Lower Pomerania there is a mountain of solid diamond which is two-and-a-half miles high, two-and-a-half miles long and two-and-a-half miles thick. Once every hundred years a little bird comes to the mountain and sharpens its beak on it, and when this big diamond mountain has been completely worn away by the bird's little beak, then the first second of eternity will be over."

"My boy," said the King, "you have answered all my questions with great wisdom, and from now on you shall dwell with me in my palace where I will bring you up as my own son."

THE TWELVE LAZY SERVANTS

IT was evening, and twelve servants, who had done nothing but dawdle from dawn till sundown, lay sprawled on the grass, boasting of their idleness.

Said the first:

"I can't be worried about anyone else's laziness; my own keeps me busy enough. To pamper my body—that is my life's work! I eat more than a little and have a great thirst in consequence. After I have eaten four big meals, I fast a short time until I feel hungry again— that agrees best with me. Early rising is not for me. I get up late and before midday I am already looking for a place to rest. If my master calls me, I act as though I hadn't heard him, and if he calls a second time, I wait a goodly while before I drag myself to my feet; and even then I walk slowly enough. That is the only way one can bear one's life."

Said the second:

"Well, my friends, it is my task to look after a horse. That is a hard job but there are ways of getting out of it. For one thing, I never take the bit out of the horse's mouth; that saves me the trouble of putting it in again every day. Then too, if I don't happen to feel like moving, I don't even bother to feed the beast—I simply tell my master the horse has eaten already. After that, as a reward for performing these heavy tasks, I give myself a good rest by lying in the oat-manger for four hours. When I wake up I stretch out one foot and move it a couple of times over the horse's body, and so in a few minutes he is curried and combed—why should one do more? But even so, this job is irksome enough."

"Yes, yes," said the third. "Why should we plague ourselves with work? No good comes of it, after all. The other day I lay down in the sun and fell asleep. It began to rain a little, but what was the use in getting up? I let it rain in God's name. At last there came a cloudburst, and such a heavy one that my hair was torn from my head and washed away; in consequence I got a hole in my head. But what of it? I put a plaster on it and all was well. Such accidents have often befallen me before, and all because of my superior laziness."

Said the fourth:

"As for me, my talents for idleness are not small either. For instance, if I am ordered to do a piece of work, I first dawdle around for an hour so that I may spare my strength. That done, I begin very gradually to look about for one or two others to help me. To these I leave the main part of the work while I really do nothing but look on; but even that is too much for me."

"That's nothing," said the fifth. "Just think, I am supposed to clean out the manure from the horses' stable and then to load it on a cart. Well, you can be sure I go about it very slowly. Little by little, I get the cart and the pitchfork in readiness, and then it is time to start in earnest. When at last I have managed to get something on the pitchfork, I only lift it up halfways, after which I rest for a quarter of an hour before I raise it all the way up and throw it into the cart. This

is slow work, but to my mind it is more than enough if I take out a cartful a day—I have no interest in working myself to death."

Said the sixth:

"Shame on you, you sluggard! With me it is different. Hard work doesn't frighten me in the least. Why? Because I simply lie down and rest for three weeks; I don't even bother to take off my clothes. Clothes are too much trouble anyway. Shoes, for instance—why take time to buckle them up? The worst that can happen is that they fall off your feet, and surely there's no harm in that. And talking about feet, if I have to climb some stairs, I very slowly drag one foot after the other up to the first step, then I stand there and count the others, so that I can figure out how many times to rest before I reach the top."

Said the seventh:

"Well, that sort of thing doesn't work with me. I have a master who watches all day to see that I do my work, but luckily he is seldom at home. Yet I do not neglect my duty, oh no! When I am called, I run as fast as it is possible to crawl, except for the times I do not care to move at all—then four sturdy men must come and push me with all their strength. Sleeping is one of my greatest accomplishments. Once I came to a place where six men in a row were lying asleep on a bench. That looked good, so I lay down beside them and slept too. In fact, I slept so well that it was impossible to wake

me, and when they wanted me back home again, they had to lift me up and carry me."

Said the eighth:

"Well, well! I see that I am the only lively fellow among us. Just to show you—if a stone lies in my path, I do not bother to lift up my legs and step over it. Why should I? It is much easier to lie down on the ground and avoid such an effort. Even if I am wet and muddy, I keep right on lying there until the sun has dried me out. At the very most I turn myself so that the sun can shine on me."

"That's the way to act!" said the ninth, "and no one is better at lying around than I am. Just listen! Today my bread lay before me but I was too lazy to reach for it even though I almost died of hunger. A jug stood there too, but it was so big and heavy that rather than go to the bother of lifting it to my lips, I suffered an agony of thirst. It was even too much for me to turn myself a little, and so I lay there all day as motionless as a log."

Said the tenth:

"Laziness is very dear to me even though it has brought me trouble and pain: a broken leg and swollen calves. This is the way it happened. Three of us were lying in the road, and just as I had my legs stretched out very comfortably, along came someone in a cart and drove right over my legs. Of course, I might have drawn my legs away, but I didn't hear the cart coming because the gnats were crawling in and out of my ears and buzzing all the time. But that couldn't be helped—it would have been too much trouble to chase the bugs away."

Said the eleventh:

"Yesterday I gave up my position. I had no desire to go on carrying my master's books back and forth—there was no end to it all day. But, to tell the truth, he didn't care to have me around any longer and so sent me packing, and that was because I had left his clothes lying in the dust until they were all moth-eaten, and a good thing too!"

Said the twelfth:

"Yes, it is too much trouble to take care of one's master's belongings. Like today, when I had to drive the cart out into the field—when I got there, I made myself a bed of straw in the cart and had a good sleep. The reins slipped from my hands and when I awoke, the horse had almost torn itself loose. The harness was gone, and the strap which fastened the horse to the shaft, that was gone too—and so were the collar and the bridle and the bit. Someone had come along and taken them all away while I slept. But how could I help it? I had to have my rest. On top of everything else, the horse had pulled the cart into a mud puddle. There it was, stuck fast, so what was there for me to do but go back to sleep again? At last my master had to come and pull the cart out of the mud himself, and take me and the horse home. If he hadn't come, I could still be lying there in peaceful slumber instead of here with you, wearing myself out talking."

LUCKY SCRAPS

ONCE upon a time there was a girl who was pretty enough, but very lazy and wasteful. At her spinning she was so careless and short tempered that whenever she found a little knot in the flax she didn't pick it out carefully as she should have done. No, she would impatiently pull out a whole handful of flax with it and throw it on the floor.

Now this idle girl had a little servant, a neat, industrious maid, who always gathered up the scraps of flax which her mistress left lying so untidily about the floor. More than that, she untangled and cleaned the scraps, spun them fine, and had a handsome dress made out of them for herself.

In the meantime, a young man in the village had asked the idle girl to be his wife, and now they were about to be married. On the eve of the wedding there was great merry-making, and when the bride-to-be saw her little servant maid prancing merrily about in her new dress, she said:

> Look how that maid does jump about,
> Dressed in the scraps which I threw out.

When the young man heard this, he asked her what she meant by it.

"Oh," said the girl, "I'm talking about my maid. There she is, dancing around in her new dress as pert as you please, but—would you believe it?—'tis made of nothing but some scraps of flax which I threw away!"

At this the young man did some quick thinking. "Well, well!" he said to himself. "It's lucky I found out in time what a lazy, wasteful girl I was about to marry." And so he gave her up, and chose the poor but industrious maid for his wife instead.

THE CAT AND THE FOX

A CAT met a fox as she walked in the woods, and because she had heard that he was a clever and important gentleman, she spoke to him in a friendly way.

"Good day, dear Sir Fox," said she, bobbing and bowing all the while. "How are you? How are things going, and how do you manage in these troublous times?"

The fox, who had a very high opinion of himself, looked haughtily at the cat from head to foot. For a long time he could not decide whether he should bother to answer her at all, but at last he said, "Oh, you poor whisker-wiper, you parti-colored fool, you pitiable starveling and miserable mouse-chaser—what's come over you? *You* dare to ask *me* how I am getting on? What have you learned during your worthless nine lives? How many tricks and arts do you know?"

"Only one," said the cat meekly.

"And pray, what may that be?" asked the fox.

"This only," answered the cat. "When the dogs are after me, I can climb up into a tree and save myself."

The fox laughed mockingly.

"Is that all?" he cried. "As for me, I am master of a hundred arts and wiles, and besides that, I have a whole bagful of tricks to help me through the dangers I encounter. And you, poor fool, have only one. How I pity you!"

Just then came a hunter with four dogs. The cat sprang nimbly up a tree, seated herself among the topmost branches where the foliage hid her well, and from there she shouted down, "Now open up your bag of tricks, Sir Fox! Open up your bag of tricks!"

But the dogs had already caught the fox and had a tight hold on him.

"Ei, ei, Sir Fox!" cried the cat. "You are welcome to your hundred arts and wiles; I am satisfied with my one. Had you been able to climb like me, you would now be as safe as I am!"

THE SOLDIER AND HIS
MAGIC HELPERS

ONCE upon a time there was a soldier who had fought valiantly for his country, but when the war was over his King dismissed him without thanks and with only a farthing's pay.

The soldier was very angry at this.

"Just wait!" he cried. "I am no fool and I won't stand for such treatment! If I can only find the right people to help me, the King shall give me all the treasures of his kingdom instead of one miserable farthing."

And so, full of fury and vexation, he strode forth into the forest, hoping to find some way of accomplishing his purpose. From the first, luck was with him, for before he had gone very far he came upon a huge man who had just pulled up six trees by the roots as easily as if they had been stalks of corn.

"A strong man always comes in handy," thought the soldier, and aloud he said, "Look, my friend. I may have a task for a sturdy fellow like you, and the two of us together certainly ought to be able to get along in the world. Wouldn't you like to come along with me?"

"Yes, gladly," said the Strong One. "But first I must take this little bundle of sticks home to my mother." With this, he took one of the trees, wrapped it around the other five, lifted the bundle on his shoulder, and carried it away.

Then he returned and traveled on with his new master. The two had gone but a short distance when they came upon a huntsman who, crouching on one knee and squinting with one eye, seemed to be pointing his gun at something.

"Whatever are you aiming at, my man?" asked the soldier, for there was no game anywhere in sight.

The huntsman said, "Two miles from here a fly is sitting on an oak tree. I was just going to shoot out his left eye."

"If you can shoot that well," said the soldier, "why bother about shooting flies? I think I'll have a better task for you by-and-by; and the three of us together certainly ought to be able to get along in the world. Wouldn't you like to come with us, Sharpshooter?"

"Oh yes," said the Sharpshooter, and he did.

As the three wandered on, they came upon seven windmills whose sails, with a great clatter, were whirling madly in the air. Yet there was no wind, neither from the north, south, east nor west, and the air was so quiet that not a leaf was stirring.

The soldier looked at the windmills and was puzzled.

"I can't understand what is turning them," said he, "for there isn't a breath of a breeze anywhere." Nor did he find the answer until they reached a tree two miles farther on. There among the branches sat a man holding a finger over one nostril while blowing mightily through the other.

"Dear me!" cried the soldier. "What are you doing up there, my man?"

"Two miles from here are seven windmills," said the Blower, "and I am blowing at them so they can turn and do their work this windless day."

"Such talent could be put to other good uses," said the soldier. "Don't you want to come with us? We four together ought to be able to make our way in the world."

So the Blower jumped down and went with them, and soon they saw a man who was standing on one leg while his other leg, which he had unbuckled, was lying beside him on the ground.

"Well now!" laughed the soldier. "You certainly have a queer way of resting your legs."

"Oh, that's not what I'm doing," said the other. "I am a Runner, and in order to stop my legs from going too fast, I have to keep one of them unbuckled most of the time. When I run with both legs, I can go faster than a bird can fly."

Soon after the Runner had joined them, they met a man who was wearing a little hat, but he had it put on so crookedly that it hung over one ear.

"Manners! Manners, my friend!" cried the soldier good-naturedly. "It is not proper to wear your hat over one ear, and it makes you look like a regular fool."

"Oh, I dare not wear it any other way," said the man, "for as soon as I put it straight upon my head, such a terrible frost comes on that the birds freeze in the air and fall dead to the ground."

"That is a great talent, Freezer, my friend," said the soldier. "I already have four good men but there's

66

always room for one more. If you will come with me, we six will go out into the world and see what we can do." And as they all traveled on together, he told them how he hoped to make the ungrateful King pay him well for his services as a soldier.

.   .   .   .   .

The six went on until they came to a town where there was great excitement over a forthcoming event. The King had proclaimed that whoever won a race against his daughter, would win her too, as a wife; but whoever lost the race, must lose his head as well.

"Ah, this comes just at the right time!" thought the soldier, and presented himself to the King, saying, "I accept the challenge of running a race with Your Majesty's daughter, only I would like to have my servant run for me."

"Very well," said the King. "But only on one condition: should your servant lose the race, both he and you shall lose your heads."

"Agreed!" said the soldier, then hurried to the Runner, helped him buckle on his leg, and said, "Be nimble now, Runner, and win for us!"

Now all was ready for the race. It had been decided that the one who could first bring some water from a distant well was to be the winner, so the Princess and the Runner were each given a pitcher. Then, at a signal, both started off, but in a twinkling the Runner was already out of sight. He ran so fast that it was just as if the wind had whistled by, and in a very short time he had reached the well, filled his pitcher with water, and was on his way back. About halfway home, however, he was overcome with drowsiness and, setting his pitcher beside him on the ground, he lay down by the roadside and fell asleep. But in order to make himself so uncomfortable that he couldn't possibly sleep long, he had taken a horse's skull which lay near-by and used it for a pillow.

In the meantime the Princess—who was indeed a fleet runner—had reached the well, filled her pitcher with water, and was on her way back, when she saw the Runner lying there fast asleep. Overjoyed, she emptied the water out of his pitcher and ran on.

Now all would have been lost had not the Sharpshooter, by great good luck, been standing at the top of the castle from where, with his keen eyes, he had seen all that had happened. Quick as a flash he leveled his gun, took aim and then, without hurting the Runner in the least, neatly shot the horse's skull out from under his head. At this the Runner awoke with a start, jumped up, and saw that his pitcher was empty and that the Princess was already far ahead of him. But, nothing daunted, he picked up the pitcher, sprang quickly back to the well, refilled his pitcher and ran back, arriving at the starting point ten minutes ahead of the Princess.

"See?" he said. "On the way back I really picked up my legs; before that it couldn't even have been called running!"

By rights the Princess now belonged to the soldier. But the King was vexed—and his daughter even more

so—that she should be carried off by a common dis-
charged soldier, so between them they took counsel as
to how they could best rid themselves of the unwelcome
bridegroom.

Finally the King said to his daughter, "I have thought
of a way out. Don't worry, these rascals won't be
around to bother us much longer!"

He went out to the six men and said cheerily, "You
shall now be my guests and shall eat and drink and
make merry together."

With that he led them to a room made of iron. The
floor was of iron, the door was of iron, and the windows
were barred with heavy iron rods. Inside was a table
laden with delicious viands—a welcome sight to the six
who had traveled so far.

"There," said the King. "Go in and enjoy yourselves
to the full." But as soon as they were inside, he had
the big iron door locked and bolted, after which he
ordered the cook to build a fire under the room—a fire
big enough to make the iron red hot.

Soon the men inside began to feel rather warm.

"Oh well," said one. "I suppose it is getting hot in
here from all this steaming food."

But as the heat became greater and greater they became worried; and when, upon trying to get out, they found the door locked and the windows bolted, they realized that the King was trying to make an end of them.

"So he wants to frizzle us up!" cried the Freezer. "But in that he shall not succeed. I'll see to that!"

Quickly he set his hat straight on his head, and immediately such a heavy frost filled the air that all the heat disappeared and the food grew cold and froze solidly to the plates. Then they sat and waited.

The King, of course, had been waiting too, but after a few hours, feeling sure that his six prisoners had been burned to a crisp, he went out to make sure that all was going as it should. Under the iron room the fire was still blazing fiercely but when the King opened the big door, a wave of chilly air blew out at him, and his six prisoners, fresh and healthy but shivering a little, stepped forth, smiling and bowing.

"Ah!" said the soldier. "We're glad to be outdoors again so we can warm up a bit! Really, it was getting so cold in there that our food froze to the dishes."

The King could not understand what had happened,

but he was still determined not to have a common soldier
for a son-in-law, so he tried another plan.

"If you will give up all claims to my daughter," he
said to the soldier, "and will take gold instead, you can
have as much as you like."

Nothing could have pleased the soldier better!

"Oh yes, my Lord King," he said. "If you will give
me as much gold as one of my servants can carry, I
will not demand your daughter as my wife. In fourteen
days I shall return to get my gold."

The King was satisfied with this and the soldier went
off and called together all the tailors in the land. For
fourteen days they sewed, making a bag of huge pro-
portions, and when it was finished, the Strong One slung
it across his shoulders and returned with it to the King's
palace.

When the King saw the huge sack he was taken
aback. "What kind of a strong fellow is that who can
carry a bundle of linen as big as a house?" he cried,
terrified at how much gold the man might be able to
carry away. Still, there was nothing for him to do but
keep his promise, so he ordered a ton of gold to be
brought. It took sixteen men to carry it, but the Strong

One picked it up with one hand and threw it into the sack, saying, "Why do you bring so little? These few crumbs are hardly enough to cover the bottom."

So more and more was brought until at last all of the King's treasure had been handed over to the Strong One who tossed it carelessly into the sack, saying, "More is needed! The sack is not yet half full."

Now seven thousand cartloads of gold had to be gathered together from all parts of the kingdom, and these too, wagons and oxen and all, were thrust into the bag. When all that was inside, there was still room for more, but the Strong One said, "Oh, I'll make an end of this and take home what I have, even if the sack isn't full."

With these words, he hoisted the sack on his back, joined his five comrades and marched away with them.

When the King saw one man carrying off the entire wealth of his kingdom, he became so angry that he sent his horsemen to pursue the adventurers and retrieve his riches. Two of the regiments soon caught up with the six, and called out to them, "You are our prisoners! Lay down that sack of gold or you will be cut to pieces!"

"What is that you are saying?" cried the Blower. "You call us your prisoners? Before I'll let that happen, I'll see you all dance in the air." He closed one of his nostrils with one finger, and through the other he blew such a mighty blast of air at the two regiments that they were blown like leaves over the mountains and through the blue air, some here, some there.

One sergeant begged for mercy, saying he had nine wounds and was a brave fellow who did not deserve such treatment. At this the Blower stopped for a

74

moment—just long enough for the sergeant to come down out of the air without injury, and then he said to him, "Now go home to your King and tell him to send some more horsemen and I'll blow them into the air too."

When the King received this message, he said, "Well, I'll have to let the rascals go—they have powers beyond mine."

As for the six adventurers, they went off laughing and singing and full of great plans for a happy future. And when they sat down to divide the contents of the mighty bag among them, the soldier said, "Now the King has paid his debt to me at last!"

THE GOOD-FOR-NOTHINGS

Roosterkin said to Hennikin, "Now is the time when the nuts are ripe. Let us go up on the nut hill and eat our fill before the squirrel gets away with them all."

"Oh yes," replied Hennikin. "Come, we will have a happy time together!"

So they went away to the hill where they ate their fill of nuts; and as it was such a bright pleasant day they stayed until it was evening. Now I don't know whether they had eaten so many nuts that they couldn't walk, or whether they wanted to put on airs—at any rate, they didn't want to go back on foot and decided to go home in a wagon. But where could they get a wagon? There was none on the nut hill.

"I will make a little wagon out of nut shells," said Roosterkin, and he did. It was a pretty wagon with a seat in front and a seat in back and with four round wheels, and it was all made of nuts.

When it was finished, Hennikin climbed into it and said to Roosterkin, "Now you can harness yourself to it and then you can pull me home."

"Oh, indeed!" cried Roosterkin. "I would rather go home on my own two legs than let myself be harnessed to it. No, that was not our bargain. I don't mind sitting on the front seat and being the driver, but to pull the wagon myself—oh no, never!"

Well, there it was. Hennikin couldn't pull it because she wasn't strong enough and Roosterkin wouldn't pull it because he wanted to drive, so what should they do? As they were noisily quarreling about this, a duck came waddling along.

"Quack! Quack! You thieves!" she scolded. "What are you doing on my nut hill? Just wait, things will go bad with you!" And with that she made a dash for Roosterkin with her bill wide open. Roosterkin, not slow, made for the duck in turn, and struck her so hard with his spurs that the duck cried out for mercy.

"Hold off! Hold off!" she quacked. "Let's all be friends and travel together. You two can sit on the wagon and I'll pull you."

So they harnessed the duck to the wagon. Roosterkin sat in the front seat, Hennikin sat in the back, the four nut wheels turned round and round, and off they went in high spirits.

"Run as hard as you can, Ducklet," cried Roosterkin. "We want to go fast!" And they certainly did. Waddle, waddle! went Ducklet. Whirr, whirr! went the nut wheels. And Rattle, rattle! went the wagon, down and down and down the nut hill.

After they had gone like this for some time they met two foot passengers, a pin and a needle.

"Stop, stop!" cried the needle.

And the pin said, "We were delayed at the inn and now it is getting so pitchy dark we can't see our way any more, and the road is so dirty besides. Couldn't we ride along with you for a bit?"

Roosterkin looked at them, then said, "Well, since

you are two such thin people, I guess you won't take up much room. So climb in, but be careful not to step on our toes with your sharp feet."

The two got in, then off they went once more, down and down and down the nut hill.

Late in the evening they came to a roadside inn, and because they did not like to travel in the dark, and also because Ducklet was getting so tired of waddling that she was falling from side to side, they decided to stop there for the night. But the innkeeper, after looking them over, thought they might be a pack of good-for-nothings who probably wouldn't or couldn't pay their way, and so he wasn't eager to have them stay.

"My house is full," he said by way of excuse. "Besides it costs something to sleep here and eat here. Have you any money?"

Well no, of course, they hadn't. "But," said Rooster-kin, "you can have the egg which Hennikin laid on the way, and you can have Ducklet too—she lays a fine big egg every day."

Then the innkeeper gave them something to eat and drink, and they had a most jolly time, after which they went happily to bed.

Early the next morning before anyone was awake, Roosterkin woke Hennikin and said to her, "Hennikin, dear. That's such a nice egg you laid yesterday, and I am hungry. Come, let's peck it open and eat it." Hennikin, too, was ready for breakfast, so together they pecked the egg open and ate everything but the shell, which they tossed into the fireplace.

Next they went to the pin and the needle who were still asleep. They took the needle by its head and stuck it into the cushion of the innkeeper's armchair, and they grabbed the pin and stuck it into his hand towel. And then, like the naughty rascals they were, they flew away over the heath as carefree as you please.

As they whizzed by over the barnyard, Ducklet, who was sleeping there, woke up too. First she shook her feathers until they were fluffy and then, finding a brook near-by, she perched upon its waters and swam swiftly away.

So now the innkeeper didn't have Hennikin's egg and he didn't have Ducklet either. But that wasn't the worst of it! Just listen and see what happened to the poor man when he got up. First he washed himself and was about to dry himself with his towel, when hui! the pin scratched him in the face. After this he went into the kitchen to light his pipe at the fire, but as he stooped over the hearth, the eggshells jumped up and hit him in the eyes.

"What's going on here?" cried the man peevishly. "Everything seems to be going against me this morning!" Angrily he sat down in his armchair but quickly he bounded up again, yelling with pain—the needle in his chair-cushion had pricked him even worse than the pin, but not in the face.

Now he was very angry and began to suspect the guests who had come so late the night before, but when he went in search of them, he found they were gone.

"Oh well," he sighed, "I'll know better next time. Never again will I take such good-for-nothings into my house. They eat much and pay nothing, and on top of that they hand out tricks and scratches instead of thanks."

THE STAR DOLLARS

THERE was once an orphan girl who had become so poor that she no longer had a room to live in or a bed to sleep in. All she had left were the clothes she was wearing and a little bit of bread which someone had given her, and now, forsaken by all the world, she wandered into the country, hoping that God, at least, would not forget her.

She had not gone far when she met a poor man who said, "I am so hungry and you have some bread. Won't you give me a little?" The girl handed him the whole piece of bread with her blessing and went on.

Next came a little boy who was crying because his head was cold, so the girl took off her cap and gave it to him. Soon there came another child—she was cold too—and to this one the girl gave her jacket; and then another, to whom she gave her little frock.

Now it was dark, and as the girl was going through a forest, there came still another child who said she was cold and begged for something to keep her warm. The girl hardly knew what to do, for she herself had nothing left but her undershirt.

"Still," she thought, "it is so dark that no one can see me," so she gave her undershirt to the child, and then stood bare and shivering in the cold. Oh, what should she do now?

The answer came from above, for suddenly something came falling out of the heavens—a shower of shiny stars which, on the way down, turned into silver dollars, hundreds and hundreds of them. And something else happened too, for although but a moment before, the girl had given away her last little garment, she now found herself wearing a new one, made of the finest linen. Into this she joyfully gathered up the silver dollars, and was rich all the days of her life.

A TRIP TO SCHLARAFFENLAND

LONG ago, in the time when houses could fly and animals could talk, when brooks burned like fire and straw was used to quench the flames—that's when I took a trip to Schlaraffenland. Well! The sights I saw there, to be sure!

In one place a plow was tilling a field all by itself with never a man nor horse nor ox to help it. A little farther on a withered old goat was carrying a hundred cartloads of lard on his back, and sixty loads of salt besides; and by a stream two greyhounds were lifting a mill, wheel and all, out of the water. Can you believe it?

I saw there a big, broad linden tree on which hot pancakes were growing, and also a stream of sweet honey which flowed like water from a deep valley to the top of a high mountain—and these were strange things.

Then I came upon some animals making bread. Four horses were threshing the grain with all their might; two goats were tending the fire; and a red cow was pushing the loaves into the oven. And I mustn't forget to tell you—in that country the goats wore boots and the cows went about on stilts. Yes, yes!

I saw even more. Two crows were mowing a meadow; two goats were building a bridge; and two doves were tearing a wolf to pieces. Then a snail came running up and killed two fierce wild lions.

The roosters in that land made not a sound, but I heard a hen crowing:

> Cock-a-doodle-do, my friend,
> Now my story's at an end!

THE THREE LANGUAGES

IN Switzerland there lived an old Earl who had an only son; but as the boy seemed stupid and unable to learn his lessons the father said to him one day, "Look, my boy. Do what I may, I can't seem to get anything into your head. Now I am going to send you off to a celebrated master to see what he can do with you."

The boy was sent to a strange town where he stayed with the learned master for a year and then came back.

"Well, my son," said the old Earl, "have you learned anything?"

"Yes," said the boy. "I have learned what the dogs say when they bark."

"Heaven have mercy on us!" cried the Earl. "Is that all you have learned? I know of another famed master; I shall send you to him."

The son went. Another year passed, and when he returned to his home, the Earl said again, "My son, you have been gone for a year and I hope you have put it to good use. What have you learned this time?"

"Oh father," said the boy, "I have learned what the birds say when they are singing."

At this the Earl became very angry and cried, "Oh, you poor fool! Here you have used up a precious year of your life and have learned nothing. Aren't you ashamed to stand here before me? I will send you to a third master and if you learn nothing this time either, I shall disown you."

The boy went to study with the third master and when he returned at the end of the year, the Earl said, "My son, what have you learned this time?"

"Oh father," said the boy, "this year I have learned what the frogs say when they are croaking."

Now the Earl's patience was at an end and, springing up in his fury and disappointment, he cried, "This is too much! To have a son who knows nothing and babbles of dogs barking, birds singing and frogs croaking—that is more than I can bear!" Then, calling some of his men, he said, "This boy is no longer my son. I drive him forth from my house and command you to lead him out into the forest and take his life." The men took him away but had not the heart to kill him, so the boy was free to try his luck in the world.

After wandering about for some time he came to a castle where he begged for a night's lodging.

"You can stay," said the lord of the castle, "if you don't mind spending the night in that old tower down yonder. But I must warn you, it is a most dangerous place, for it is full of wild dogs who bark and howl fearfully night and day. It is said that they thirst after human blood and at certain hours demand a live man whom they gobble up at once."

At the mention of dogs the boy pricked up his ears. "What, only a pack of dogs?" he said. "I'm not afraid of them, no matter how much they may bark or howl. All I ask is a bit of food to throw at them when I get there."

The lord of the castle was glad enough to help him out, and gave him some meat to take with him.

As the boy entered the tower, the dogs did not bark, did not howl, did not bite; instead, they ran toward him in a friendly manner and wagged their tails joyously. They ate the food he had brought them and when he stretched himself out on the floor to sleep, the dogs lay peacefully near-by and did not hurt a hair of his head.

The next morning when he returned to the castle, everyone was astonished to see him still alive and unharmed. When they asked how he had managed to quiet the furious beasts, he said, "Oh, the dogs told me in their own language why they live there and why they bark and howl all the time. It is only because they are enchanted and must guard the wonderful treasure which is hidden under the tower. They can't rest until it has been dug up and taken away."

"But how can the treasure be found?" asked the people.

"Oh, the dogs told me that too," said the boy, and with this he went back to the tower. When he returned he had a treasure chest filled with pure gold. From then on there was no more barking and howling in the old tower; the dogs disappeared and the land was quiet and safe once more.

•   •   •   •   •

After a time the boy became restless and decided to go to Rome. On the way he passed a marsh in which a number of frogs were croaking loudly. At this the boy pricked up his ears. "Now I wonder what those frogs are talking about," he thought.

He sat down and listened, but when he heard what they were saying he became quite thoughtful and solemn. Then he got up and went on his way.

As he entered the city of Rome, there was great excitement and sorrow everywhere. The Pope had just died, and the Cardinals were full of doubt and worry because they didn't know whom to name to succeed him. At last they came to an agreement, saying, "That person toward whom a miracle is shown shall be the new Pope." At that very moment the young Earl stepped into the church, and immediately two snow-white doves appeared and alighted on him, one on each shoulder.

"That is the miracle, the holy sign!" cried the Cardinals joyfully, and asked the young Earl then and there whether he would consent to become the new Pope. The boy was overwhelmed by the honor but, fearing that he was not worthy of it, he hesitated. But the two doves leaned over and whispered in his ear that he must accept; and so at last he said yes.

Then he was anointed and consecrated, and thus it came about that what the frogs had told him and which had made him so thoughtful and troubled came true— for they had told him that he would become Pope.

After this he was asked to sing a Latin mass but, as he had never been able to master that language, he would have been in a bad predicament, had not the doves sitting on his shoulders, then and evermore, told him what to say.

THE STRAW, THE COAL, AND
THE BEAN

AN old woman who had gathered a mess of beans
for her supper was building a fire on her hearth. In
order to make it burn up quickly she threw on a handful
of straw, but as she did so, a piece of straw slipped out
of her fingers and dropped to the floor. Then, as the
woman was emptying the shelled beans into the soup pot,
one of the beans, too, fell unnoticed to the floor where
it rolled along until it lay beside the straw. By this
time the fire on the hearth was blazing merrily when,
pop! a glowing coal bounced out and landed on the
floor beside the straw and the bean.

The straw was the first to speak.

"My dear friends," said he, "how did you happen to get here?"

The coal said: "Oh, I made a quick jump out of that fireplace, and a good thing too, or I should certainly have been burnt to ashes."

"As for me," said the bean, "I also was lucky enough to escape with a whole skin, but if I hadn't rolled away in the nick of time, I should have been mercilessly boiled to death in the bean-soup along with the rest of my bean-friends."

Then the straw said: "Things went badly with my companions too. Just think, without the least regard for their feelings, the old woman allowed my straw brothers to go up in fire and smoke. Sixty of them she grabbed in a bunch and brought to a bitter end, but I, luckily, was able to slip through her fingers and save myself from such a fate."

"Well," said the coal. "Here we are, alive and hale and hearty. What shall we do now?"

And the bean said: "This is the way I look at it. Since we three have escaped death so miraculously, I believe we should stay together and be good comrades. But it is too dangerous here with fires and bean-soup

96

and all, so I think we should get out of this place and wander in some foreign land."

This plan pleased the other two, so they all started off together. By-and-by, as they reached the open country, they came to a little brook; but although they looked upstream and down, they could see no bridge anywhere.

"Now what shall we do?" asked the bean. "I could never jump across all that water."

"Nor I," said the coal.

But the straw soon thought of a good plan to help them. "I'm long enough to reach from one bank to the other," he said, "and if I lay myself across the water like a bridge, then you two can walk over on me."

So that was what he did—laid himself across the brook so that his head rested on one shore and his feet on the other. The bean, who had a cautious nature, made no move to go; but the coal, who was a bit hasty and hot-headed, tripped boldly upon the newly-made bridge. But when she reached the middle and heard the water rushing and roaring beneath her, she became frightened and stood motionless, not daring to go any further. Ah me, that was certainly the wrong thing to do! The little coal was still rather hot, and while she stood hesitating, the straw caught fire, then broke in two and sank into the water. As for the poor little coal, she slid off the burning, breaking bridge, hissed wildly as she fell into the water, and was gone.

The bean, who was still on shore and had been laughing at all the tumbling and slipping which was going on, now found she couldn't stop, and so she laughed and laughed until she burst.

That was the end of her merriment, and it might have been the end of her too, had it not been for a wandering tailor who stopped to rest himself beside the little brook. When he saw the little bean in such a pitiful state, the kindhearted fellow whisked out his needle and thread and sewed her neatly together again.

Now the bean was whole again, but she looked somewhat different than before because the tailor had used black thread in stitching her up. And that is why, since that time, all beans have a black seam down their middle. Look at one some time and you'll see this is true.

THE WISHING TABLE, THE GOLD DONKEY, AND THE CUDGEL-IN-THE-SACK

Long ago there was a tailor who for years had worked hard in order to raise his three sons. Every day he sat cross-legged on his table and stitched away, but now as he was getting old he said to his oldest boy, "It is time you went out into the world to learn an honest trade so that you can support me in my old age. I haven't much to give you," he continued, "only a farthing and a pancake to start you on your way. The rest is up to you."

The boy went forth. On the first day he ate his pancake, on the second he spent his farthing for food, and on the third he said to himself, "Now you must find work, no matter what it is, otherwise you will starve."

Luckily, before the day was over, he found someone who needed help—a little gentleman who lived in a nutshell, but who was tremendously rich all the same.

"If you will not disobey me," said this tiny lord, "I will pay you well. All you need to do is to herd my cattle on the hill every day for a year. But heed my words! At the foot of the hill is a house from which issues the most lively dance music, but this house you must never enter."

And the boy said, "I will herd your cows well and will make it my business to stay away from the house of music."

He found it easy enough to keep the first part of his promise, but not so the second. Every day while he was herding cows on the hill, such sweet and lilting melodies floated up from the house below that the boy was almost beside himself with the desire to see what was going on there.

At last, one day long before his year was up, he was unable to control his curiosity any longer. "I'll just go a little nearer," he thought, "so as to hear the music better." But the nearer he went the gayer sounded the music, and before he knew it, he was in the forbidden house, dancing and singing with the merry folk who lived there.

When he came back that night the little lord came out of his nutshell and looked at him sternly. "You have disobeyed me," he said. "I hired you to work, not to dance and make merry; therefore I must send you away. But since you have done your work well in the time you were here, you shall not go forth empty-handed."

So saying he handed the boy a little table. It was not much to look at, for it was plain and made of ordinary wood, but it had one remarkable quality. Whenever anyone set it down and said, "Table, be decked," the good little table went into a sudden flurry, and in the next instant, there it was, spread with a snowy cloth and decked out with elegant dishes and silverware. Besides that, it was laden with platters and bowls of luscious food—roasted and baked and boiled—and, with this, a glass of wine so clear and red and sparkling that it warmed one's heart to look at it.

The boy thanked the tiny lord for this wonderful wishing table, and to himself he thought: "Now I will have enough for all my days. And my old father, he will be glad too, for with this handy table we'll never want for food, and the poor old man can at last give up his tedious work of tailoring."

So with a light heart he set out for home, and whenever or wherever he felt hungry, whether in field or forest or meadow, he took the table from his back, set it on the ground and said, "Table, be decked," and there was his meal, ready to eat.

One night, when he was but a few miles from home, the boy stopped at an inn. It was filled with many jolly guests who greeted him cheerily and invited him to dine with them. But the boy said, "Oh no, I don't want to take those few morsels out of your mouths; instead, I would like to invite you as my guests."

The people, seeing that he looked far from rich, laughed heartily at what they thought was surely meant for a joke. But they stopped laughing and stared in astonishment when at his command, "Table, be decked," they saw the simple wooden table transformed into a festal board piled high with such delicacies as the innkeeper could never have provided, and from which a most savory smell rose to greet their nostrils. And what surprised them most of all was that as soon as any dish became empty, a full one would immediately appear in its place.

The innkeeper, meantime, stood in a corner and watched all this in goggle-eyed wonder. "Such a cook would come right handy in your household," he said to himself; and after everyone else had gone to bed he lay awake for hours wondering how he could get this wonderful table for himself. At last he remembered that in his rummage room he had an old table which looked just like the magic one. He rose and fetched it and then, creeping softly into the boy's bedroom, he quickly and quietly exchanged it for the wishing table.

Early the next morning the boy, suspecting nothing, picked up the table, hung it on his back and went on to his home. He was greeted with joy by his father.

"And have you brought anything back with you to help me in my old age?" asked the tailor.

"That I have," said his son. "See, here it is." And lifting the table from his back, he set it on the floor.

The old tailor looked at it from all sides, then said, "But this is just an old poorly-made table!"

"So it may seem," said the boy, "but it is a wonderful wishing table all the same." And after telling his father about its remarkable powers, he added, "Now let us invite all our friends and relatives. They shall feast as they have never done before, for my table will set forth enough food for everybody."

When all the people were assembled for the promised feast, the boy set down his table in the middle of the room and cried, "Table, be decked!"

Dozens of eyes watched eagerly but nothing happened. The table did not bestir itself and remained as bare as any ordinary table which does not understand magic words. At this the guests, who were angry at having to go home as hungry as they had come, mocked him and called him a liar; while the poor boy, realizing now that he had been tricked by the innkeeper, hung his head in shame. As for the old father, he had to go back to his tiresome tailoring once more.

In the meantime the tailor's second son had gone off to look for work. After eating his pancake and spending his farthing for food, he too found his way to the lord who lived in a nutshell. His experience was much like that of his brother. After herding the lord's cows for a while, he was lured from his work by the lively music which floated up to him, and tempted him to dance in the forbidden house. For this he was sent on his way by the lord, but not without a reward for his service.

His present was a donkey.

"It is a peculiar kind of donkey," explained the tiny lord, "which neither draws a cart nor carries a sack. But he is useful all the same, for if you place him on a cloth and say, 'Bricklebrit,' the good animal will spew forth gold pieces for you, as many as you need."

"Well now, that is a fine thing!" cried the boy, and

after thanking the lord for this remarkable gift, he set out for home. After traveling two days he came to an inn, the same one—although he did not know it—at which his brother had been tricked out of his wishing table some time before. As he was leading his donkey into the barnyard, the innkeeper came to take it to the stable, but the boy said, "Oh, don't trouble yourself, I'll tie up the beast myself, for I must know where he stands."

"Hm!" thought the innkeeper. "I suppose he's so poor he must look after his own animal. Such a one will spend but little and is not worth my time." But when the boy handed him two gold pieces and asked to be given a good dinner, the astonished innkeeper opened his eyes wide and was glad enough to scurry around and dish up the best food he could find.

After his meal, which was indeed a good one, the boy said carelessly, "How much more do I owe you?" and the innkeeper, eager to get all he could out of such an easy-going customer, neatly doubled the reckoning and said, "Two more gold pieces."

The boy felt in his pocket but found that his gold was at an end. "Wait a minute, Sir Host," he said, "I'll have to go and get some more money," and with that he whisked the tablecloth off the table and walked away with it. This made the innkeeper so curious that he stole out after his strange guest, but since the boy took care to bolt the stable-door after himself, the man had to be content with peeping through a knothole in the door. When he saw the boy spreading the tablecloth under the donkey, his eyes fairly popped out of his head with wonder; and when he heard the boy say, "Bricklebrit," and saw a shower of gold pieces falling down on the cloth, he thought, "Well now, that's the easiest way of making money I've ever seen. Such a purse would not come amiss!"

This put an idea into his head, and that night when everyone was sleeping he went into the stable, led the gold donkey away, and tied up one of his own donkeys in its place. Early the next morning the boy untied the donkey and led it away, never guessing that it wasn't his own.

By midday he reached his home where he was greeted with open arms by his father.

"And what have you brought to help me in my old age?" asked the tailor.

"Oh, nothing but a donkey," said the boy.

"As to donkeys," said the old man, "there are enough of those around here already. A good goat would have pleased me better."

"Yes, but this is no ordinary donkey," said the son. "He is a magic one, and when one lays a cloth under him and says 'Bricklebrit' he spews out nothing but gold pieces. Just call together all our relatives and I'll make you all rich."

"That suits me well enough," cried the old tailor, "for then I won't need to torment myself with snipping and stitching and patching any more," and with this he ran out and called together all their relatives.

When the company was assembled for the promised treat, the boy brought the donkey into the room and placed him on a cloth which he spread out on the floor. Then he cried, "Bricklebrit!" but no gold pieces fell, and this showed that the animal was nothing but an ordinary donkey who was ignorant of the art of making gold. The relatives, who were bitterly angry at having to go away as poor as they had come, mocked the poor boy, while he, realizing that the innkeeper had tricked him, pulled a long face and bore his disappointment as best he could. As for the old father, he had to betake himself to his needle again and toil for his living as before.

·   ·   ·   ·   ·

In the meantime the third boy had been sent forth with his pancake and his farthing, and with him things went much the same as it had with his brothers. He too chanced upon the little lord who lived in a nutshell, and was soon herding cows for him. The only difference between him and the others was that he, when going

out upon the hill, stuffed his ears with cotton so that he might not hear the music floating up from the forbidden house. In this way he was able to serve out his full year, and for that the tiny lord gave him a present—a knapsack with a cudgel in it.

"Well," said the boy, "I can easily carry the sack on my back and it may be very useful to me, but why should the cudgel be in it? That only makes it heavy."

"I'll tell you why," said the lord. "If anyone does you any harm, just say, 'Cudgel-out-of-the-sack,' and it will leap out and pummel him so soundly that he won't be able to move for eight days, and it won't stop either, until you say, 'Cudgel-into-the-sack.'"

The boy thanked the little lord, hung the knapsack on his back and set out for home and, whenever anyone came too near him or tried to attack him, all he had to do was cry, "Cudgel-out-of-the-sack!" and instantly the cudgel would leap out of the sack and deal out a shower of blows.

After two days of traveling the boy reached the inn where both his brothers had stayed, but since they had told him in a letter how the innkeeper had cheated them out of their wonderful magic gifts, he was on his guard against the rascal. Seating himself on a bench, he laid his knapsack on the table before him and began telling about all the wondrous things he had seen in the world.

"Yes, yes," he said, "it is not unusual to come across a wishing table or a gold donkey or suchlike marvels— all good things which I by no means despise—yet these are nothing compared to the remarkable treasure which I am carrying about with me in this sack!"

At this, as may be imagined, the innkeeper pricked up his ears. "Good heavens, what in the world could that be?" he thought. "No doubt the sack is filled with jewels; and in all justice they should be mine, for all good things go by threes." And from that moment his head held but one idea—that of getting the treasure for himself.

When bedtime came, the boy lay down on a bench, placing the sack beneath his head for a pillow. But the innkeeper did not go to bed. He waited until he thought the boy was sound asleep, then tiptoed up to him and began pulling very gently and carefully at the sack, hoping to get it out and to put another one in its place.

But the boy had been waiting for this for a long time. He was not asleep at all, and just as the innkeeper was about to give a final tug, the boy jumped up and cried, "Cudgel-out-of-the-sack!"

Well! Out came the cudgel, pounced upon the innkeeper, and thumped him on his back until the seams of his coat were ripped from top to bottom. In vain he cried for mercy. The louder he yelled the harder the cudgel beat out the time on his back, until at last the boy said, "Now then! You had better give back the wishing table and the gold donkey you stole from my brothers, or else we'll make you dance some more."

"Oh no!" cried the innkeeper humbly. "I'll gladly give back everything if only you'll make that confounded goblin get back into the sack."

So the boy cried, "Cudgel-into-the-sack," after which, leaving the innkeeper to brood over his misdeeds, he went to bed.

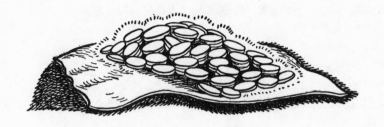

Early next morning, with the three wonderful treasures in his keeping, the boy went back to his home. When his father asked him what he had brought with him from his travels, he said, "A fine thing, father. See? A cudgel in a sack."

"A cudgel!" cried the tailor. "It was hardly worth your while going out into the world for that. You could easily have cut one for yourself out of any tree."

"But not one like this, dear father," said the boy. "If anyone wishes to harm me, all I have to do is to call my precious cudgel out of the sack and it will lead him a sorry dance, and it won't stop, either, until he prays for fair weather. And just think! In that way I have got back the wishing table and the gold donkey which the thievish innkeeper took from my brothers. Now let's send for them both, and for all our relations besides, and we'll get together enough food and gold for them all!"

The old tailor, remembering the experiences of his two other sons, was doubtful about the whole matter; nevertheless he called everyone together. Then the donkey was brought in, and the brother to whom he belonged set him on a cloth and cried, "Bricklebrit!" And, of course, since he was really the Gold Donkey, all went well and the gold pieces rained down upon the cloth like a cloudburst, nor was there an end to it until everyone had as much gold as he could carry. (I can see by your face that you would gladly have been there yourself!)

Next, the little table was brought into the room, and the brother to whom it belonged set it down on the floor and cried, "Table, be decked!" And, of course, since this was the real Wishing Table, it understood the magic words and did as it was told. Whish and whirr! there it was now, decked out with a clean white tablecloth, exquisite china and silverware, and loaded down with the

114

most delectable food imaginable. Then such a grand and merry meal took place as the tailor had never known in all his born days, and the relatives stayed and enjoyed themselves far into the night.

All were happy and contented, but none more so than the old father, for now at last he was able to lock up his needle and thread, his yard-measure and tailor's goose, and to live in ease and comfort with his sons for the rest of his days.

THE TAILOR WHO WENT
TO HEAVEN

Do you know the story of the tailor who went to Heaven?

It was a beautiful day in Heaven—so beautiful, indeed, that the good God decided to go for a pleasant stroll in the heavenly garden. With him went the apostles and the saints—all of the holy folk except Saint Peter, who had to stay behind and see to it that no one entered the heavenly portals in the meantime.

Well, not long and there came a knock at the door.

"Who is there?" asked Saint Peter. "And what do you want?"

"I am a poor honest tailor," said a fine, polite voice, "who begs for entrance into Heaven."

"Oh indeed!" said Saint Peter. "As honest, no doubt, as a thief on the gallows. I happen to know that you are inclined to be light-fingered, and that many a time you have tweaked off a bit of cloth and kept it for yourself. No, you can't come into Heaven; the Lord has forbidden me to let anyone enter while he is away."

"Oh, do have pity on me!" cried the tailor. "To pick up a few little scraps of cloth which have fallen from the table all by themselves, that's not stealing, and surely not worth mentioning. Just look, I am limping and my feet are full of blisters from walking so far— I couldn't possibly go back all the way. If you will only let me in, I will do all the worst work around here. I'll carry the little babies and wash their diapers, clean and scour the benches on which they have been playing, and even mend their little clothes."

At this, Saint Peter's heart softened and he opened the heavenly gate a crack—just wide enough for the shriveled-up tailor to squeeze through.

"But you must sit behind the door," Saint Peter warned him, "and be very quiet so that when the Lord returns he may not see you and become angry with you."

This the tailor did obediently enough, sat behind the door quiet as a mouse, didn't move and didn't say a word. But as soon as Saint Peter had gone outside the door, he got up and walked around, peeping inquisitively into every corner of Heaven to see how things were arranged there.

At length he came to a place where many exquisitely beautiful chairs were standing about. The most beautiful of these—an armchair of pure gold, set with sparkling gems—stood in the very center of the room. It was also much higher than the other chairs, and before it stood a golden footstool. This was the Lord's armchair upon which he was wont to sit when he was at home, and from which he could see all that was happening on the earth below. Of course, our little tailor did not know this, and after looking at the golden seat for a while, he thought, "That armchair pleases me more than all the rest." There he stood, gazing at it and wondering about it until at last, unable to control his curiosity any longer, he climbed up and sat in it. As soon as he had done so, he could see all that was happening on the earth below.

And what did he see, this impertinent little tailor? He saw many things, but what caught his eye was a homely old woman who, while washing some clothes beside a brook, stealthily picked out two veils which she then quickly laid aside for herself.

"Oh, the thievish creature!" cried the tailor, and so infuriated was he by this sight that he picked up the golden footstool and flung it right through Heaven •at the old woman down below.

Now he first realized what he had done, and since he knew he could not get the footstool back again, he slipped quietly down from the armchair and out of the room. Once more he took his place behind the door where he sat quietly as before and behaved as though he had never moved from the spot.

When the Lord returned from his walk, he did not notice the tailor behind the door, but when he went to sit on his golden armchair, he saw that the footstool was missing. He asked Saint Peter what might have become of it but the good saint said he didn't know.

"Have you allowed anyone to come in here while I was gone?" the Lord asked then.

"I know of no one who has been here," replied Saint Peter, "except a lame and footsore tailor, but I made him sit behind the door, and there he is still."

"Bring him here," said the Lord, and our little tailor came.

"Was it you who took away my golden footstool, and if so, what did you do with it?" asked the Lord.

"Oh, Lord," answered the tailor eagerly, "down on the earth I saw an old washerwoman stealing two veils, and in my wrath over such wickedness I flung the footstool at her."

"Oh you knave!" said the Lord. "Were I to judge

as you have judged, how do you think things would have gone with *you* all this time? Indeed, were I to treat the sinners on earth as you have done, I should long ago have had no chairs, no benches, no seats—yea, not even a single oven-fork—left up here. Henceforth," he continued, "you can no longer stay in Heaven but must go again out beyond the gate; there you must get along as best you can. Up here no one shall mete out punishment but I alone, the Lord!"

So Saint Peter had to open the heavenly gate and send the tailor out of Heaven, but the little fellow, because his shoes were so torn and his feet so full of blisters, did not go back to the earth again. Instead, he took his staff in his hand and hobbled along until he came to a place called "Wait-a-While" where the good soldiers sit and make merry.

PRESENTS OF THE LITTLE FOLK

A TAILOR and a goldsmith were traveling together, and one evening, just as the sun had slipped behind the mountains, they heard the sound of distant music. Clearer it came, and louder, as the two walked on; but it was no ordinary music, this they felt sure of. It had a weird, sweet charm, but a rousing power too, for as they listened, the two travelers lost all feeling of fatigue and found themselves walking with a new and easy vigor.

After the sun had vanished, the moon rose big and round and full. Briskly the two strode on until at length, guided by the strains of magic music, they came to a grassy knoll on which many wee men and women were whirling round and round in a dance of joyous abandon. They sang most charmingly, too, in tiny bell-like voices, and this was the mysterious music the travelers had heard.

The two, half-hidden by leaves and bushes, stood spellbound by what they saw. In the very middle of the whirling circle sat an old man somewhat taller than the rest. He was wearing a coat of many colors and had a long white beard which hung down to his waist. When he spied the two strangers standing there, he beckoned them to join him, and as he did so, the tiny dancers willingly opened their circle so that the newcomers might enter it.

The goldsmith, who was humpbacked, and like many such, rather pert and bold, stepped fearlessly into the circle; the tailor, who was shy and afraid, held back at first, but when he saw how merrily things were going, he took heart and came too. Then the circle closed around them and the wee people went on singing and dancing with the wildest leaps and bounds imaginable. As for the old man, he now began to act strangely. Taking a broad-bladed knife which hung at his girdle, he whetted it smartly and then, when it seemed sharp enough, cocked his head and looked at the newcomers

124

this way and that. The goldsmith and the tailor were terrified at this, but there was no time to worry and even less in which to get away. Before you could count three the old man had grabbed the goldsmith and—swish!—swash!—he had sheared off the poor man's hair and beard. In a trice he did the same thing to the tailor. This done, he gave them each a friendly tap on the shoulder as though to tell them they had done well not to struggle against him. Then he pointed to a heap of coals which lay close by and, with further signs and gestures, invited the two to fill their pockets with them.

The goldsmith and the tailor were puzzled at this. They did not understand how the coals could be of any use to them in their travels, but remembering the old man's big sharp knife, they obeyed. Then, with friendly bows, they went off to look for a night's lodging.

As they walked away from the grassy knoll the magic music grew fainter and fainter, but they could still hear it and could still see the fairy folk dancing gaily in the moonlight. Looking back, they walked on. As they reached the valley, a clock in the neighboring monastery struck twelve, and in that moment the singing ceased, the little folk vanished, and the fairy knoll lay silent and empty in the silvery moonlight.

The two travelers found an inn. Here they lay down on their straw beds and covered themselves up with their coats, but in their weariness they forgot to take the coals out of their pockets. The heavy weight pressing upon their bodies awakened them earlier than usual the next morning, and when they reached into their pockets to empty them of the burdensome black lumps, they could scarcely believe their eyes. Their pockets were no longer filled with coals but with pure gold instead! And another good thing had happened—during the night their hair and beards had miraculously grown back again in all their former fulness.

Now they were both rich, but the goldsmith, who was naturally greedy, had filled his pockets with a double amount of coal, so that he was twice as rich as the tailor.

Well, a greedy man, even though he has much, is apt to yearn for more, and so it was with the goldsmith.

"What do you say, little snipper?" he said to the tailor. "Let's tarry here another day, and tonight we'll go back to the Old One on the knoll and get us another load of treasure."

"No," said the tailor. "I have enough; I am satisfied. Now I can become a master tailor, set up a little shop of my own, marry my agreeable object (as he called his sweetheart), and so I will be a happy man. But,"

he added, "as we are friends and have traveled so far together, I'll stay on with you another day and keep you company."

That evening the goldsmith, after slinging several bags over his shoulders so that he might be able to stow away great quantities of coals, went alone to the fairy knoll. As before, he found the carefree little people singing and dancing in the moonlight, and as before, the old man beckoned to him, shaved his head and his chin and then, pointing to the heap of coals, made signs to him to take as much as he pleased. Since this was just what the goldsmith was waiting for, he lost no time in getting at the task. Greedily he stuffed his pockets and all the sacks he had brought, then staggered blissfully under his heavy load back to the inn. Then, lying down on the straw bed beside the sleeping tailor, he covered himself with his coat and with all the coal-filled sacks besides.

"What if they do press burdensomely on me during the night?" he thought. "I'll bear it patiently, happily even, for it will be more than worth it in the morning." And so with sweet anticipations for the morrow, he fell asleep.

The next morning as soon as he awoke, he jumped up and began emptying his pockets. He found nothing but coal. Next he looked into the sacks, one after the other—they held nothing but coal and coal and coal!

He was bitterly disappointed.

"Still," he thought, "I have yet my gold from the night before, and so I am twice as rich as the tailor." But when he went to get the gold, he found that all this had been turned back into coal again.

There he stood, the greedy goldsmith, his hands and clothes all black with coal dust, looking dazedly about him. In despair he beat his head with his hands, only to find that his head was still bald and smooth—his hair had not grown back during the night as it had before. With his beard it was the same—that was still gone too. All this was bad enough but it was not the worst! In addition to the hump on his back he now had another on his chest as well, and realizing that he had been punished for being so greedy, he burst into tears.

At this the good tailor awoke from his sleep. When he heard his friend's story he comforted him as best he could, saying, "You were my companion on our long travels. You are still my friend and shall share my riches with me."

The tailor kept his word, but the poor goldsmith had to walk around the rest of his life with a hump back and front, and had to keep his bald head covered with a cap night and day.

THE THREE SPINNERS

THERE was once a lazy girl who hated spinning from the bottom of her heart and, no matter how much her mother talked and scolded about it, the girl would not, would not spin. At last one day the mother lost her temper and spanked the girl until she cried out at the top of her lungs—cried and wailed so lustily that the Queen, who happened to be passing by, heard it and came in to see why she was being punished.

The mother, ashamed to admit her daughter's laziness, said quickly, "Oh, the child is a great trial to me! All she wants to do is spin and spin and spin, and I am too poor to buy her so much flax."

"Indeed!" said the Queen. "Then let her come with me and she can spin as much as she likes. There is plenty of flax in my palace, and besides, the humming of the wheel delights me, and I am never happier than when I hear the pleasant sound of spinning."

The mother was heartily pleased with the plan, so the Queen took the girl to her palace where she showed her three rooms filled from floor to ceiling with unspun flax.

"Here, my child," said the Queen. "Now you can spin to your heart's content, and when you have spun all the flax in these three rooms you may marry my eldest son. It doesn't matter that you're poor; such industry as yours is dowry enough."

And so she went, leaving the girl to herself with a spinning wheel, three rooms full of flax and her own thoughts which, as you may be sure, were far from happy.

"Oh, oh!" wailed the girl. "I can never spin all that flax. No, not even if I lived to be a hundred years old and worked at it from morning till night." And so, weeping bitterly, she sat down, folded her hands in her lap and did nothing. The next day it was the same, and the third, too, except that in the evening the Queen came to see how things were going. When she saw that the girl had not spun even the tiniest wisp of flax, she asked why this was so.

"Oh," said the girl, "I have been so homesick that

I haven't been able to do a thing."

"I can understand that and am willing to forgive you," said the Queen, "but tomorrow you must begin in earnest." And she left the room.

The girl, not knowing what to do, got up and looked sadly out of the window; as she did so, her glance fell upon three old women coming along the street. But what odd-looking creatures they were, to be sure! The first had a broad flat foot; the second had an enormous, drooping underlip which hung down over her chin; and the third had such a big clumsy thumb that it was beyond all belief.

As the three old women neared the palace window and saw the girl's troubled face peering out at them, they stopped and asked her what was the matter, and after hearing the girl's tale of woe, they offered to help her.

"If you will invite us to your wedding," said they, "and if you will promise not to be ashamed of us but will introduce us as your cousins, and if you will let us eat at your wedding table, why then we will spin up all the flax for you, and that in a very short time too. Will you promise us this?"

"With all my heart!" said the girl. "Just come right in and begin your work. I'll run down and open the door for you."

This she did, and pushing the flax to one side so as to make room for them, she brought her new friends into the first chamber.

And now the three odd creatures sat down and began their spinning. It was a sight to see! The first drew out the thread, and with her big flat foot she trod the treadle; the second, with her thick drooping underlip, licked and moistened the thread; while the third, with her big broad thumb, twisted the flax and struck the table with her finger, and every time she did so, a skein of finely spun yarn dropped down to the floor—and in this way the flax was spun up like magic.

Yes, things were going well now, and the girl was highly pleased. Whenever the Queen came to see how she was getting on, the girl quickly hid her three homely helpers out of sight, then happily displayed the great masses of neatly spun flax; and the Queen, seeing it, could not praise the girl highly enough.

The three spinners worked on—treading, licking and twisting away until at last, with the three rooms full

BUT WHAT ODD-LOOKING CREATURES THEY WERE, TO BE SURE!

of flax spun into wondrously fine yarn, they rose and took leave of the girl.

"But don't forget!" they warned her. "Don't forget your promise to us. If you will do as we've asked you to do, it will bring you luck."

When the Queen saw the three empty rooms and the heaps of fine yarn, she began making preparations for the wedding. As for her son, the Prince, he was much pleased at the prospect of getting such a clever industrious wife, and praised the girl mightily.

Then the girl said, "I have three cousins who have been very kind to me, and I do not want to forget them now that I am so fortunate and happy. May I invite them to my wedding and let them sit with us at the table?"

"Yes, indeed. Why not?" said the Queen and the Prince.

And so on the day of the wedding the three old women appeared, bowing and smiling with pleasure. They were dressed in the most remarkable finery— yards and yards of frills and ribbons and ruffles—which, however, did not hide or lessen their ugliness in the least. They looked homelier and odder than ever, but the new bride greeted them in the most friendly fashion. "Welcome!" she said. "Welcome to my wedding, dear cousins."

The bridegroom meantime was staring at them in astonishment.

"Really," he said to the girl, "I can't imagine how you ever came to have such very homely cousins!"

Then, full of curiosity, he stepped up to the three old spinners, and to the first he said, "From what did you ever get such a big flat foot?"

"From treading," said she, "from treading."

"And you," he said to the second, "from what did you ever get such a thick drooping lip?"

"From licking," said she, "from licking."

Then the Prince turned to the third and said, "From what did you ever get such a big broad thumb?"

"From twisting flax," said she, "from twisting flax."

At this the Prince became alarmed and said, "Well, if that's what spinning can do, my beautiful bride shall never again touch a spinning wheel!"

And so the girl was rid of the hateful flax-spinning forever.

THE SIX SWANS

Years ago, when there was still much magic in the world, there lived a good King. His wife was dead but he had seven children, six boys and a girl, whom he loved above all else in the world.

One day while hunting in a big forest, the King lost his way. He looked for a way out but found none. The farther he went, the more hopelessly lost he became, and as the evening drew near he feared he might starve or be eaten by wild beasts before anyone could find him. Full of despair, he sat down to await his fate, whatever it might be, when he saw an old woman with a waggly head approaching him.

The King went up to meet her, saying, "Dear woman, I am hopelessly lost in this dense and endless forest. Can you not show me the way out?"

"That I can, my Lord King," said the Old One. "But only on one condition will I do so. If you do not fulfill it, you will never get out of this forest and must die miserably of starvation."

"What is the condition, then?" asked the King uneasily, for there was something uncanny, almost witch-like, about the old woman.

"I have a daughter," said the Old One, who was indeed a witch, "—a daughter so beautiful that it is beyond all belief, a maiden so wise and clever that she is well worthy of being your wife. If you will make her your Queen, I will show you the way out of the forest."

The King, seeing that this was the only way of escaping with his life, promised; after which the old woman led him to her little cottage where her daughter was sitting by the fire. The young woman arose as though she were expecting him, and the King saw that she was, without doubt, beautiful beyond compare. After he had taken the maiden up on his horse, the Old One showed him the way out of the forest, and before long they had reached his castle where the wedding was soon held.

It was not a happy wedding for the King, however,

for although his new wife was very beautiful, there was also something cold and heartless about her which made him shudder every time he looked at her. From the moment he had first set eyes upon her in the forest, he had felt this way about her and so, fearing that she might not take kindly to his children, he had never told her about them. Instead, he had taken them to a lonely castle in the midst of a forest, where he knew they would be safe and happy and where he could visit them every day. So well hidden was this castle, and so confusing was the path leading to it, that the King himself could never have found his way there had it not been for a Wonder Ball of yarn which a Wise Woman had once given him. This Wonder Ball, when tossed out ahead of him, unrolled itself and miraculously showed him the way to the castle.

It was not long before the Queen became curious about the King's frequent absences.

"Why do you spend so little time here with me," she asked him, "and where is it you go every day?"

But the King would not tell her.

"Very well," she thought, "then I'll find out for myself. I'll ask the servants. They know everything that

141

goes on, and if I give them enough money, they'll tell me."

She was right. The servants, upon seeing the money she offered them, told her that the King had a flock of little ones whom he visited faithfully every day, and told her, too, about the Wonder Ball of yarn and where it was kept. From that time on, the Queen's one thought was to get rid of the children who took up so much of her husband's time, and soon she was busy with her plans.

Now the truth of it was that this Queen—who, after all, had a witch for a mother—was an enchantress herself, and it was this which made her so strange. Alas! she was not only strange but wicked as well, and so was the plan she now began to work upon.

First she made some little shirts of white silk, into each of which she stitched her wicked witchery. Then one day, after the King had gone off on an all-day hunting trip, she took the enchanted shirts and, with the help of the Wonder Ball of yarn, made her way to the hidden castle.

The children, seeing some one in the distance, thought it was their father coming to visit them and rushed out joyfully to meet him. The Queen, losing no time, threw one of the little white shirts over each of them, and in a moment they were changed into beautiful white swans which flew away over the treetops.

Now the wicked Queen was satisfied and, tossing the Wonder Ball ahead of her, went home in high spirits, thinking, "Well! Now there's an end to the little nuisances."

But she was wrong, for not all the children had run out to meet her. By a lucky chance, the little girl had remained inside the castle and so the Queen knew nothing about her.

On the following morning, when the King went to visit his children as usual, he was puzzled to see only the little girl running out to meet him.

"And where are all your little brothers?" he asked.

"Oh papa," said the girl sadly, "they're gone. I was watching them from the window and all at once they were boys no more, just swans; and then—Flrrr! Flrrr! Flrrr!—they flew away over the treetops and left me all alone."

"It can't be," said the King. "You must have been dreaming, child."

"Oh no, it's true, papa," said the girl. "See, here are some of their feathers which fluttered down as they flew away."

The King could not imagine what had happened, and was afraid to leave his little daughter alone in the castle lest some harm might befall her too. But when he wanted to take her with him, the girl said, "No, don't take me away—I'm afraid of my stepmother. Let me stay a little longer." And since the King did not know where to keep the child so that his wife would not see her, he said, "Well, just for one night then, and by tomorrow I'll find a new, safe home for you."

So he went away feeling deeply troubled and sad. But the little girl said to herself, "I'm going to look for my six dear brothers and when papa comes back he'll be so glad I've found them again!"

144

Donning her hood and mantle and little red boots, she took a loaf of bread against hunger, a small jug of water against thirst, and a tiny red chair to rest on when she was tired. Then she went straight into the forest. All day she walked and the next day too, eating nuts and berries when her bread gave out, and refilling her jug with water from the clear cool woodland streams. Sometimes she rested on her little red chair, and at night she slept among the branches of a big protecting tree.

At last, toward the end of the second day, as she was plodding wearily through the forest, she came upon a little woodland hut. The door was open, so she walked

in and looked around. Here was a neat room, spotlessly clean, but no one was in it. Along the wall were six little beds, soft and snowy white. How inviting they looked, and what a pleasure it would have been to rest her weary little self on the downy feathers!

"But they are not my beds," she thought. "I have no right to sleep in them." So she crawled under one of the beds and lay down on the hard floor, intending to spend the night there. But just before sunset she heard a whirring, rustling sound, and when she peeped out from under the bed she saw six graceful white swans flying into the room through the windows. Landing lightly on the floor, they puffed and blew at one another until they had blown off all their feathers, then they stripped off their swan skins as if they had been shirts. Now they were swans no longer but six young boys instead; and the girl, knowing well enough that these were her six lost brothers, crept from her hiding place and stood before them laughing merrily.

The six boys stared at her but said not a word.

"What's the matter?" asked the girl. "Aren't you glad to see your little sister?"

"Oh, yes we are!" said they. For a fleeting moment their eyes lit up with joy, but in the next their faces clouded over with sorrow.

"Don't be sad!" cried the little girl. "I've come to take you home."

The six shook their heads. "No, we can't leave," said they.

"Well then, I'll stay and keep house for you."

Again they shook their heads.

"No, that can't be either," said the oldest. "This place is a shelter for robbers. If they find you here they will kill you."

"But here you are, six strong boys," said their sister. "I'm sure you can guard me from them."

"No," said the second. "It is only for a quarter of an hour after sunset that we are allowed to be boys. All the rest of the time we are swans and have to fly around in the fields and woods, hiding from the hunters who are always trying to shoot us."

At this the little girl burst into tears. "Then I will free you!" she cried.

Her brothers looked mournfully at each other but were silent.

"Tell me, please," wept their sister, "is there no way?"

"Only one," said the oldest boy, "and that is too hard; we could never ask it of you."

"But what is it?" she asked.

"For six years," said the boy, "you would not be allowed to laugh or talk, and during that time you would have to sew six magic shirts for us out of tiny star-flowers. Yet if you were to say a single word or give one fleeting smile, all would be lost. Oh no, little sister, that's too much to ask of anyone, much less of such a gay and lively creature as you are."

As the boy finished speaking, the quarter hour was just at an end, and the six brothers, enchanted once more, were turned into swans and had to fly away.

"But I'll do it!" said the little girl to herself as she watched her poor dear swan-brothers disappear among the trees. "I'll do it gladly if it will only make them real boys again."

Leaving the little hut, she wandered far into the middle of the forest where she found a big hollow tree in which she spent the night. The next day, after gathering thousands and thousands of star-flowers, she climbed back into the hollow of the tree and began to sew. It was no easy task—the flowers were so fragile they kept tearing and falling apart. Often after she had spent weeks making one sleeve it would go to pieces after all.

It was very lonely for her. There she sat day after day, week after week, month after month—all through the sweet spring, the sunny summer, the chilly fall and the dreary winter. One year passed; two, three, four and five years passed. Still she sewed and sewed, said not a word, and never, never laughed. Nor did she feel like laughing any more—she felt too sad and worried about her poor enchanted swan-brothers, flying around in danger of being shot at any moment.

Her clothes became faded and tattered from the sun and the wind and the rain; moss grew up so thickly

149

around her that she could scarcely be seen. But her face
was as sweet and fair as ever and her hair, though
tangled and matted, shone like gold in the sun.

One day—the fifth year had just come to an end—
a King came galloping through the forest and was
astonished to find a winsome face peeping forth from
the leaves and mosses of a tree.

"Who are you, fair one?" he asked. "Are you real?"
She said nothing.

"Wouldn't you give me one little smile?"
She did not smile, but sewed and sewed.

"What are you sewing then?"
She only shook her head.

"Ah, perhaps she is a foreign maid," thought the King.
He talked to her in other languages—all the languages
he could think of—but the girl remained silent as a fish.
All the same, unsmiling and speechless as she was, she
looked so sweet and modest and charming that the King
fell deeply in love with her and felt he could not live
without her.

"Dear maiden," he said, "you please me more than
anyone I have ever seen. Will you come with me and
be my bride?"

"WHO ARE YOU, FAIR ONE?" HE ASKED

With a happy light in her eyes the girl nodded her head, and the King, overjoyed, plucked off the moss, tore away the weeds, bent back the branches and lifted her down. Then, wrapping his mantle about her and placing her on the saddle before him, he took her to his castle and married her.

He was very happy with his new bride, even though she never laughed nor talked; but his mother was displeased with his choice.

"My son," she cried, "have you lost your senses? Couldn't you find someone better than a ragged beggar-girl for a wife? And then she's deaf and dumb besides. She can't help that, to be sure, but at least she could smile once in a while. Never to laugh—that's a bad sign; and as for her sewing those shirts out of star-flowers from morning till night, it isn't natural. She's a witch surely!"

For a long time the King paid no attention to his mother's words, but she nagged and nagged at him and invented so many bad stories about the innocent girl that in the end he was forced to believe her; and one day, sad and heavy of heart, he consented to have her burned as a witch.

But it was now six years to the day since the girl had stopped talking and laughing. The shirts were almost ready too, and as she was led to the brush-pile, she was carrying five perfect flower shirts on one arm and was trying to finish the left sleeve of the sixth. But, just as the King's mother was ready to set fire to the brush-pile, the last moment of the sixth year was at an end, and—

Flrrr! Flrrr! Flrrr! Flrrr! Flrrr! Flrrr! there was a soft whirring sound in the air, and down fluttered the six swans. They settled beside their sister so that she was able to toss the star-flower shirts over their heads. As soon as the shirts touched them, their swan skins fell off and there they stood, six handsome hearty lads, looking just as they had before, except that the youngest, upon whom the unfinished shirt had fallen, had a beautiful swan's wing in place of his left arm.

Joyfully the girl kissed them all in turn and then, running to her King husband, she said, "At last I can tell you the truth, for now I am able to talk like anyone else. You will see that I am innocent and not a witch at all."

When he had heard the story, the King was happy be-

yond words, and planned a big festival to celebrate the
reunion of the Princess and her brothers.

I wish we—you and you and you and I—had been there
too. That would have been a party indeed!

THE QUEEN BEE

THERE were once two Princes, one as thoughtless as the other, who went out in search of adventure. But they fell into such a wild, wasteful way of living that before long they had used up all their money and had no way of getting home again. At this their younger brother, who was rather simple and was called Duncehead, went out to look for them. He found them, too, but when he wanted to join them in their travels, they scoffed at him.

"What!" they cried. "How can a simpleton like you hope to make your way in the world when we two clever ones couldn't get on?"

But Duncehead went with them after all, and one day as all three were walking along they came upon an ant-hill.

"Ah, here is sport!" cried the two thoughtless brothers, for they wished to amuse themselves by stirring up the ant-hill and watching the little ants as they hurried frantically about, carrying their little eggs to safety.

But Duncehead said, "No, leave the poor little creatures in peace. I can't bear to have them disturbed."

The three traveled on until they reached a lake which was full of swimming ducks.

"Come, let us catch some of them," said the two thoughtless ones. "Then we can roast them and eat them. That will be fine!"

But Duncehead said, "No, let us leave the poor creatures in peace. I can't bear to have them killed."

Again they traveled on, and before long they came to a bee's nest in a tree. Hundreds of bees were flying about the nest in which there was so much honey that it overflowed and trickled down the tree trunk.

"Come, let's build a fire under the tree," said the two thoughtless ones. "That will smoke out the bees and choke them, and then we can help ourselves to all the honey we want."

But Duncehead stopped them again, saying, "No, leave the little creatures in peace. I can't bear to have them burned."

At last the three brothers came to a castle. They soon

saw that it was an enchanted one, for everything was silent in it and not a living soul was anywhere about. In the stables stood many horses which had been turned to stone, and in the castle itself were many stone statues which had once been people. Full of curiosity, the three lads walked through the halls and chambers of the castle, but wherever they went it was the same—there was no sign of life anywhere, and a cold stony silence hung over everything.

At length they found a door which was fastened with three locks. After trying in vain to open these, they spied a little shutter in the middle of the door. They opened the shutter and, as each in turn peeped through it, they saw a room in which a little grey mannikin was sitting at a table.

They called to him once and then once more, but the little old man did not hear them. They called a third time, and now the little grey fellow got up, unlocked the door, stepped out and stood before them. Not a word did he say, just led them silently to a richly set table; then, after motioning them to eat, he disappeared.

The three adventurers, who had become very hungry by this time, set to with a will, and when they had finished,

the little grey man appeared once more. With beckoning fingers he showed each of them to a separate sleeping chamber, after which the three, weary with their day's wandering, slept soundly all night.

Early the next morning the little grey mannikin came to the eldest Prince, and beckoning silently, led him to a stone tablet on which were inscribed three tasks by means of which the castle could be freed from enchantment.

Of the first task it was written:

"Under some moss in the forest lie the Princess's pearls, a thousand in number. These must be found, but if by sundown even one is missing, the seeker shall be turned to stone."

After reading this, the eldest Prince went into the woods. All day he searched, scratching around in the earth and tearing up moss by the handfuls, but by sundown he had found only a hundred pearls; so he was turned to stone.

The following morning the second brother went to the forest in search of the pearls, but he fared little better than the first. He found only two hundred pearls; so he too was changed into stone.

Now it was Duncehead's turn to go in quest of the treasure. Out into the forest he went and busily, oh so busily, he searched under the moss, but the work was so slow and the pearls so hard to find that he sat down on a rock and began to cry. "Ah me!" he thought. "Now I too will be turned to stone."

But while sitting there with his head drooping unhappily toward the ground, he saw something crawling in the grass at his feet. It was the Ant King, followed by five thousand smaller ants, the very ones whose lives he had saved only a few days before.

"You were kind to us," said the Ant King. "Now we

will show our gratitude by helping you." And even before he had finished speaking, the five thousand ants had begun crawling under the moss and were dragging forth hundreds of pearls which they piled in a neat heap on the ground. When all the pearls had been gathered—and there were exactly a thousand of them—Duncehead thanked his friendly helpers, then hurried back to the castle to see what the second task might be.

"In the bottom of a lake not far from here," so ran the words on the stone tablet, "lies the key to the Princess's chamber. If by sundown the key is not found, the seeker of it will be turned to stone."

"Alas!" thought Duncehead as he started out, "how can I ever hope to see a key at the bottom of a lake?"

But it was the same lake which he and his brothers had passed a few days before, and on it, swimming happily, were the very ducks whose lives he had saved! As he neared the lake, all the ducks swam toward him.

"You took pity on us when our lives were in danger," said they. "Now we will show our gratitude by saving you from a dreadful fate."

At this, one of the ducks dived down into the water and when it came up again it was carrying the key on its bill. Duncehead thanked the ducks happily and then went back to see what the third task might be.

It was the hardest of all.

"In a chamber in the castle," so read the words on the stone tablet, "the three daughters of the King lie fast asleep. Of these, the youngest and sweetest must be chosen, but he who makes the wrong choice shall be turned to stone."

Duncehead found the chamber without much trouble, but when he saw the sleeping Princesses his heart sank, for all three looked exactly alike! Only in one way did they differ from one another—all of them, before going to bed, had eaten some kind of sweet. The oldest had eaten a piece of sugar, the second a bit of syrup, and the youngest a spoonful of honey; but since Duncehead had no way of knowing which Princess had eaten the honey, he did not know which to choose.

As he stood there trying to make up his mind, a Queen Bee—the very one whose hive he had saved from burning—flew into the room.

"You saved me and my family from a terrible death," said the Queen Bee, "and now I will save you from being turned into stone."

Flying from one Princess to another, the bee tasted the lips of each until she came to the one who had eaten the honey. "That is the youngest and sweetest Princess," said the Queen Bee, and flew away.

So now, helped by the friendly creatures who were grateful for his kindness, Duncehead's life was saved and the spell which had fallen over the castle was broken. In the stables the horses lost their stony shapes and came back to life, while in the castle all the people who had been imprisoned in stony slumber woke up and were alive once more.

Even the two thoughtless brothers were freed from their stony state and were real live lads as before. The oldest married the oldest Princess, the second married the middle Princess and Duncehead, to his great joy, won the hand of the youngest and sweetest of the three and was made King of all the land.

THE HEDGEHOG AND THE RABBIT

THIS is a lying story, my children, but it's true all the same, for my grandfather who told it to me used to say: "It must be true, my child, or else how could one tell it, after all?"

But this is the way the story goes:

It happened on the Buxtehuder Heath on a Sunday morning at harvest time just as the buckwheat was coming into flower. The sun was climbing up into the heavens, a morning breeze blew gently over the stubbles, larks trilled in the sky, bees buzzed in the buckwheat, and everybody was going to church in their Sunday best—in short, all creatures, great and small, were contented, and the hedgehog was too.

This hedgehog, he was standing there in his doorway with his arms crossed on his chest, pointing his nose to the wind and singing a little tune—that is, as good or bad a tune as a hedgehog might be expected to sing on a lovely Sunday morning.

While he was humming contentedly to himself in this charming fashion, a thought came into his head. "While my wife is busy washing and brushing the little ones," he thought, "I might as well go for a Sunday stroll and take a look at my turnip patch." The turnip· patch was in the field next to his house and belonged to a farmer, but because the hedgehog and his family had fallen into the habit of eating there, they had come to think of it as their own.

Well, no sooner said than done. The hedgehog closed the

house-door after him and sauntered down the road. But just as he reached the blackthorn bush which grew outside the turnip patch, he met a rabbit who was out on the same business—that is to say, he had come to see how *his* garden, the cabbage patch, was getting along.

Bowing and smiling, the hedgehog wished the rabbit a pleasant good morning, but the rabbit—who was a grand gentleman in his own community, and most haughty about it too—this rabbit did not return the hedgehog's neighborly greeting. Instead he said with a mocking air, "Hm! And how do you happen to be running around in this field so early in the morning?"

"It's such a pleasant Sunday," said the hedgehog. "I'm just out for a little stroll."

"A stroll!" jeered the rabbit. "I should think you could put your legs to better use than that!"

This remark wounded the hedgehog beyond words, for he was very sensitive about his legs which were short and somewhat crooked. So now he bristled up and cried in fury, "Oh yes? You must think that your legs are better than mine!"

"That's what I think," said the rabbit calmly.

"Yes, that's what you think," cried the hedgehog, "but

I'll wager that if we ran a race, *I'd* win it."

"That's a joke!" cried the rabbit. "You with your stumpy little legs! However, if you are so bent on making a fool of yourself, I'll take you on. What shall be the prize for the winner?"

"A golden coin and a bottle of brandy," said the hedgehog.

"Agreed!" cried the rabbit. "Get in line and let's go."

"Oh, no hurry about it," said the hedgehog carelessly. "I haven't even had breakfast yet. You can get the prizes; I'll be right here on the spot in half an hour."

With that he left, for the rabbit was satisfied with this plan.

On the way home the hedgehog was busy with his thoughts. "That rabbit will depend upon his long fleet legs," he thought. "My legs are—well, they're neither long nor fleet but I'll beat him to it all the same. He may be a grand gentleman, yes—but he's an old muddle-noddle; and I, I'm not as stupid as I may look."

Upon reaching home, the hedgehog said to his wife, "Come, hurry and get yourself ready. I need you out in the field."

"What's going on, then?" asked his wife.

"Oh nothing much. I told the rabbit I would run a race with him, and I'd like to have you around while it's going on."

"My heavens, man!" cried his wife. "Are you out of your head? How could you ever hope to win a race against a rabbit?"

"No words, wife!" cried the hedgehog sternly. "That's my business. Don't poke your nose into men's affairs. March along now! Are you ready?"

What could the wife do? She had to obey whether she wanted to or not, and as they waddled along side by side, the hedgehog said to her, "Now listen well to what I'm telling you. In this big field, that's where we'll run our race, the rabbit and I. See these long deep furrows?"

"Yes," said his wife, "but—"

"Silence!" cried her husband, and then continued: "The rabbit of course will run in one furrow and I in the next, and we'll start over there at the upper end of the field. Now, all you have to do is to sit at the *lower* end of *my* furrow. Understand? Don't move from that place; just sit there quietly, and when you hear the rabbit coming along, just pop up your head and say, 'Here I am already!'"

So that's the way it was done. The hedgehog left his wife hiding in the lower end of his furrow and—one, two, three!—off they went like a whirlwind down the field. That is, the rabbit did. The hedgehog only ran a few steps, ducked down in his furrow and crouched there, out of sight and quiet as a mouse.

The rabbit ran for his life, his ears flapping in the wind. He thought he was doing remarkably well, but as he neared the lower end of the field, someone cried, "Here I am already!"

The rabbit couldn't believe his ears, and when he looked over into the next furrow, he could hardly believe his eyes either. What he saw, of course, was the hedgehog's wife, but since she looked exactly like her husband, the rabbit couldn't tell the difference.

"Well, it's the hedgehog all right," he thought. "All the same, I don't like the looks of the whole thing." Then,

still panting for breath, he cried, "Another race! The
other way round!" and off he went, so fast that it was a
wonder his ears stayed on his head. The hedgehog's wife
didn't move; she stayed quietly in the lower end of the
furrow as her husband had ordered her to do.

In a twinkling-and-a-half the rabbit had returned to the
upper end of the furrow, yet there sat the hedgehog, calling, "Here I am already!"

The rabbit, now almost out of his head with fury, cried
wildly, "Another race—the other way round!"

"As often as you wish, for all I care," said the hedgehog.

Back and forth went the rabbit, forth and back, then
back and forth again—but always when he reached the end
of the furrow, it was the same old story: there sat the
hedgehog, calling, "Yoo hoo! Here I am already."

Seventy-three times he tried it, this racing rabbit, but
at the seventy-fourth time he had to give up. His legs
folded up under him, his ears flopped sideways over his
head, and then, with his breath coming in weary gasps, he
sank down in his furrow and lay there with closed eyes.

The hedgehog picked up the prizes and called his wife
out of the furrow, saying, "The race is over and, as you

see, I won it." Then they both went home together in great delight, and if they're not dead, they're living there still.

Yes, that is the way the story goes, my children, and it must be true, or how could it be that, ever since that time, no rabbit in the Buxtehuder Heath has dared to pass a remark about a hedgehog's legs? Yes? No? Well, what do you think about it?

THE EARTH GNOME

A RICH King had three daughters who were the joy
of his heart. The pride of his heart was a large palace park
filled with beautiful flowers and handsome trees of many
kinds. He was especially proud of his trees, and one in
particular, an apple tree, was his favorite. So highly did
he prize it that he allowed no one but himself to touch it.

"Anyone who lays hands on this apple tree will regret
it," he said, "and whoever picks even one apple from it
will be sent one hundred fathoms under the ground."

No one touched it, the apple tree flourished and every
fall its fruit became redder and fuller.

One year there came a harvest when the tree was so full of beautiful red apples that the tree was ready to break with the load, and its boughs hung down to the ground. The three young Princesses walked under the tree every day to see if the wind had blown down an apple but never, never did they find one. At last the youngest Princess became so hungry for one of the round rosy apples that she said to her sisters, "Our father loves us too dearly to wish us at the bottom of the earth. I think he only meant that for strangers."

With this she plucked an apple and bit into it.

"Oh, taste this, my sisterkins," she said. "Now have I never in all my life tasted anything so good!"

The two other Princesses also bit into the apple, whereupon all three sank down into the earth so deep that no rooster ever crowed after them.

That noon when the King went out to fetch his daughters to the midday meal he could not find them. He called for them but they did not answer. He sent servants to search the palace grounds—the children were not found. At last, grieved and troubled, he sent out a proclamation to his people.

"Whoever can find and bring back my three beloved

daughters," he said, "shall have one of them for his wife."

At this hundreds of people went searching through the land, for the three girls were beloved by all because they had always been so friendly to everybody and were so beautiful besides.

Among the many who went forth on the search were three young hunter boys. For seven days they walked: looked here, looked there, found nothing. On the eighth day they came upon a big castle and, finding its doors open, they walked in and looked around. From one beautiful room to another they wandered until they came to a great dining hall where stood a table set with sweet and savory food, still so warm that it was steaming. The three hunter boys, now hungrier than ever, sat down and looked at the tempting dishes, hoping that someone might come and invite them to dinner. For half a day they sat there but no one came. Then they searched from one end of the castle to the other but in it no living being was to be seen or heard.

When they returned to the dining hall and found the food still warm and steaming, they could bear it no longer. They sat down at the table and ate their fill. All went well—no one stopped them, the food tasted good, and they felt delightfully refreshed after the meal. Then, feeling strong and full of courage once more, they made plans to continue their search for the three Princesses.

"Since no one seems to be living in this castle at present," said the first, "we may as well make this our home for a while."

"And every day we'll draw lots for one of us to stay here and watch the castle," said the second, "while the other two go out on the search. Do you agree, Dull Hansl?"

"Yes," said the youngest brother. Dull Hansl was not his real name but the two older brothers always called him that because they considered him dull and simple and because they didn't like him very well.

When the lots were drawn, it came out that the oldest brother would be the one to stay at home the following day.

.   .   .   .   .

The next morning the two younger brothers rose early, ate a good breakfast at the steaming table, then set out to try their luck.

The oldest brother stayed behind and kept careful watch over the castle but nothing happened until noontime. And

174

then, who came? A little, little fellow—a gnome—came begging for a bit of bread to eat. The hunter took some bread off the table and cut a big slice all around the loaf. But when he handed it to the gnome, the little creature let it drop out of his hand and said, "Oh, now my bread has fallen to the floor! Wouldn't you please be so good as to pick it up for me?"

The hunter stooped down to pick up the bread, when whish! the gnome picked up a stick, grabbed the hunter by the hair and gave him a good beating. When he had done that, the gnome disappeared.

The next day it fell to the lot of the middle brother to stay at home but he fared no better than the first. That evening after the others had returned, he called his oldest brother aside and said, "Well, how did things go with you yesterday?"

"Oh, things went badly with me," said the oldest. "There came a little fellow who asked for bread; when I handed it to him he dropped it, and when I tried to pick it up for him the rascal thrashed me soundly."

"Just so it happened to me today," said the middle brother, "and what it all means, I don't know. But let's not say a word about it to Dull Hansl—he may as well

175

have his troubles like the rest of us." And to this the oldest brother agreed.

On the third day, of course, it was Dull Hansl's turn to stay at home. There, at noontime, came the little gnome again, begging for a morsel of bread. Dull Hansl cut a slice from the loaf which was lying on the table and handed it to him. But the little fellow let it drop and said as before, "Oh, there goes my bread! Wouldn't you be so good as to pick it up for me?"

"What?" cried Dull Hansl. "Can't you pick it up yourself? If you don't even want to take that much trouble for your daily bread, you don't deserve any either."

"You *must* do it!" shrieked the gnome, his small face red with fury.

For an answer Dull Hansl picked up the little rascal and gave him a good thrashing.

"Stop! Stop!" yelled the gnome. "Let me go now, and I'll tell you where the three Princesses are."

"That's better!" said Dull Hansl and stopped. "Now sit down and tell me your story."

"I am an Earth Gnome," said the little one, "and of us there are more than a thousand. We live down inside of the earth and that is how I happen to know where the lost

176

Princesses are. They ate one of their father's forbidden apples and so they sank one hundred fathoms down into the earth. And there they are still, inside of an old well in the King's palace garden. But it is an old forgotten well; there is no water in it."

"Thank you," said Dull Hansl. "And tomorrow you can take me and my brothers to this well, and then we will rescue the Princesses."

"No!" cried the gnome. "No, no! You must say nothing of this to your brothers. They do not like you and will not deal honestly by you. If you wish to free the Princesses, you must do it without your brothers."

"But I could never do it all alone," said Dull Hansl.

"If you do as I say, you will get other help," said the gnome. "Now then, get a big basket and let yourself be lowered into the well. Take a bell with you and don't forget your hunting knife, you'll need it! You'll need it for this reason: in the well are three rooms, and in each room there is one of the Princesses who has to sit there and comb the fleas out of the hair of a dragon with many heads. Those many heads you must cut off."

When the gnome had said these words he disappeared.

That evening when the two older brothers returned they said, "Well, Dull Hansl, how has it gone with you to-day?"

"Oh, so far so good," said Dull Hansl. "All day I have seen no living creature, only such a little man who came and asked for a piece of bread and then let it drop to the floor. When I wouldn't pick it up for him, the little thing began to scold me. Such a bold little rascal! But I showed him a thing or two. I thrashed him roundly until he begged me to stop. After that he became right friendly and even told me where the three Princesses are hidden."

At this the other two turned green and yellow with anger, but then they said, "So where are the Princesses now?"

And did Dull Hansl tell them? Ah yes, he did. He forgot all about the gnome's warning and told them everything. At this his brothers were well pleased and began making plans for the morrow.

.   .   .   .   .

The next morning, after eating a hearty breakfast at the steaming table, all three journeyed forth to the King's orchard, and as soon as they reached it they drew lots as to who should first go down into the well. Again the lot fell to the oldest. So he took the bell and climbed into the basket, saying, "But as soon as I ring, you must pull me up immediately."

The two younger boys, after lowering the basket, waited and listened. It was not long before they heard a tinkling down below, so they pulled the basket up. The oldest brother stepped out of the basket, looking very pale. "I didn't like it down there," he said.

Next the middle brother tried it, but he, too, tinkled the bell before he was halfway down. When he stepped out of the basket he was trembling. "I saw no use in going all the way down," he said. "I think that gnome was lying anyway."

Now it was Dull Hansl's turn to go down.

"He won't go far," said the oldest brother after they

had lowered the basket. "We'll hear his bell tinkle in a minute."

But they were wrong, for Dull Hansl allowed himself to be lowered to the very bottom of the well, one hundred fathoms under the ground. It was dark down there and far from pleasant, but Dull Hansl, seeing a door, took his hunting knife, stepped out of the basket and listened at the keyhole.

All he heard was a loud threefold snore.

"That is not the snore of a human being," he thought. "No doubt it comes from one of the dragons, and I may as well get to work on him."

Slowly he opened the door and peered in. There in a cave-like room was a dragon, sound asleep and snoring mightily. His heads, three of them, were resting on the lap of the oldest Princess, and she was busily combing his hair.

Dull Hansl, losing no time, raised his hunting knife, and:

Whack! Whack! Whack!

the dragon's three heads were off and lying on the floor. The Princess jumped up, hugged and kissed him, and

180

thanked him for freeing her. So grateful was she that she even took off her stomacher of pure gold and hung it around his neck.

Now Dull Hansl opened the door of the second room, and there he saw a medium-sized dragon, also sound asleep and snoring even louder than the first. This one had seven heads and his hair was being combed by the second Princess. Dull Hansl raised his hunting knife and:

Whack! Whack! Whack!
Whack! Whack! Whack!
WHACK!

off went the dragon's seven heads and fell to the floor. The second Princess jumped up and thanked him, and then Dull Hansl went on and opened the third door. In that room was the youngest Princess combing the hair of a very big dragon. He was a dragon with nine heads and he was sleeping soundly and shaking the earth with his nine-fold snores.

Dull Hansl was glad to see him so sound asleep and lost no time. He raised his hunting knife, and:

Whack! Whack! Whack!
Whack! Whack! Whack!
Whack!
Whack!
WHACK!

off went the nine heads of the biggest dragon. At this the three Princesses were so happy that they crowded around Dull Hansl and hugged and kissed him without stopping.

Now that all the Princesses were free it was time to get them up to the earth again. Dull Hansl placed the oldest Princess in the basket and tinkled the bell so loudly that his brothers above heard it and pulled her up. Next the second Princess was drawn up, and then the third.

Finally it was Dull Hansl's turn to be pulled up but

now, at last, just as he was about to step into the basket, he remembered that the gnome had warned him against his brothers.

"First I will try them out to see if they mean to do right by me," he thought, and so he picked up a heavy rock and put it in the basket. Then he tinkled the bell.

The two older brothers tugged at the basket until it was halfway up to the earth, then cut the rope so that the basket fell back into the well. It made a loud thud, at which the two brothers were pleased, for now, thinking that they were rid of their youngest brother, they planned to claim the reward for themselves. But before they consented to take the Princesses back to their father, the two false brothers made them promise they would never tell a living being how they had been saved.

. . . . . .

While the brothers were presenting themselves to the King as his daughters' rescuers, Dull Hansl was wandering sadly around in the three rooms in the bottom of the well.

"Now what shall I do?" he said. "The rope is cut, my brothers are gone—I shall be left to starve down here no doubt."

He saw a flute hanging on the wall. "Oh flute," he said,

"why are you hanging there? No one would be merry enough to play a tune on you in this dismal place!"

He looked at the dragons' heads too, saying, "And you can't help me either."

All night he walked, back and forth, forth and back, and did it so many times that the earth floor became smooth and shiny from his footsteps. But in the morning, as he

passed the flute again and again, he began to get an idea. "That flute seems to be there for something," he thought. "I'll blow on it and see what happens."

So he took the flute and blew on it. And what happened? Dozens of little earth gnomes appeared from all around him! With each note he played, another gnome came; and he blew and blew on that flute until the room was crammed with the tiny creatures.

"What is your wish?" asked the many little gnomes in many little voices. "We are here to do your bidding."

"Oh, I would dearly love to be back up on the earth in the good daylight," said Dull Hansl.

184

"It shall be done," said the many little gnomes. With this, they all took hold of him, one little gnome on each hair of his head, and in that way they flew up to the earth into the good daylight with him. And as soon as Dull Hansl was up there, the gnomes vanished.

Dull Hansl now went to the King's palace, arriving there just as the oldest brother was about to be wed to the oldest Princess. He appeared before the King and his three daughters, but as soon as the three Princesses set eyes on their true rescuer, they all fell into a faint.

The King became very angry at the poor boy.

"Throw this newcomer into the dungeon!" he cried to his servants. "See—he has hurt or bewitched my dear daughters, the sorcerer!"

At this Dull Hansl was taken away and locked up in the dungeon. But as soon as the three Princesses recovered their senses and heard what had happened, they rushed up to the King and asked him to change his mind about the newcomer.

"Please free him, father," said the first Princess.

"He did not hurt us—he is good," said the second.

"But why do you say this?" asked the King. "Have you seen him before?"

The Princesses looked at each other, and then the youngest said, "That is something we cannot tell you, father. We promised never to tell it to any living being."

"If you have promised that," said their father, "I will not ask you to tell me. But why don't you go out into the kitchen and tell it to the stove? That is not a living being."

The three Princesses ran out into the kitchen, closed the door, and told the stove that it was Dull Hansl, and not his two brothers, who had freed them and killed all the dragons. And did the stove hear it? I don't know. But the King, who stood outside the kitchen door, heard every word of it, and I am sure you can guess the rest!

The two brothers were punished for their wickedness and Dull Hansl was allowed to choose one of the Princesses for his wife. He liked them all, but he chose the youngest because she was just his age, and so they were married and lived happily ever after.

THE THREE LUCKY ONES

A<small>N</small> old man with three sons called them to his bedside and gave them each a present.

To the first he gave a rooster.

To the second he gave a scythe.

To the third he gave a cat.

"I am far along in years," said the father, "and I want to make sure that you will be well provided for after I am gone. To be sure I have no money to leave you, and what I am giving you may seem of little value, but remember this, my sons: anything is worth much or little depending upon what use is made of it. All you need to do is to look for a land where that same thing is unknown—then your future is as good as made. Try it, and you will see!"

After the old man had died, the eldest son took his rooster and went forth into the world, but wherever he went roosters were already well known. In the towns he could see them from afar, perching on the tips of church spires and turning briskly in the wind; while in the villages and all over the countryside he could hear them crowing in every barnyard. Alas! It did not look as though he would ever be able to make his fortune with a rooster.

At last, however, he chanced upon an island where lived a race of people who had never heard of roosters; nor had they ever learned to divide the day or the night into hours. By the sun they could tell whether it was morning, midday or evening, but if they awoke during the night they had no way of knowing whether the night had just begun or whether morning was near at hand.

"Ah, this is the place for my rooster!" thought the boy. So he called the people into the village square and held up his rooster, saying, "Just look what a proud animal he is, flaunting a ruby red crown upon his head and wearing spurs on his feet like a knight! In the dark of the night he will thrice call out the time, and when he calls for the

190

last time it will soon be time for the sun to rise. But if you should hear him crowing in broad daylight, prepare yourself for a change in the weather."

The people, well pleased with this novelty, crowded around and looked at the bird; and that night none went to bed. All stayed awake to listen as the rooster called off the time in a clear loud voice; at two, at four and at six o'clock. When they asked the boy if his wonderful animal were for sale and how much he might want for it, he replied, "About as much gold as a donkey can carry."

"A trifle for such a treasure!" cried the people and paid him gladly enough.

When the boy returned to his home with his donkey and his gold, his two younger brothers listened with wonder and interest to his tale.

Said the second one, "Well, well, I think I will take myself off too, and see if I can get rid of my scythe as neatly as that."

He wandered far and wide but it did not look as though he would be likely to make his fortune after all, for wherever he went he met peasants and laborers who were carrying scythes as good as his. At last, however, he chanced upon an odd little island where, as luck would have it, lived a race of people who had never in their lives seen or heard of a scythe. These people, when their grain was ripe, dragged out big cannons, set them in front of the grain stalks and shot them down, for they had no way of cutting them. But this was always an uncertain matter, for some of the shots went too high and missed the grain completely; others went too low and hit the ground instead of the stalks; while still others hit the grain-heads instead of the stalks, and in this way much of the grain was scattered and lost. Aside from that, it made a dreadful noise, and all were dissatisfied with the method.

But now, here came this boy with a long, sharp, curved instrument; and there he stood in the field, mowing down the grain so neatly, so swiftly and so quietly that the people watched with open mouths and popping eyes. When they asked the boy whether he would sell the marvelous tool, declaring themselves willing to pay whatever he might wish for it, he said, "Oh, about as much gold as a horse can carry."

" 'Tis a mere nothing for so much," said the people and paid it gladly.

Thus the second boy went home without his scythe, but with a horse and a load of gold.

When the third son saw this he said, "Well, now I must find the right place in which to dispose of my cat."

At first his experience was much like that of his two brothers. As long as he stayed on the mainland, there was no business to be done—there were cats everywhere, not only enough, but always too many. He could have had all he wanted for nothing!

At last he reached a river from which he could see an island. At this his hopes rose, and he made haste to reach it. What luck! It was an island where cats had never been heard of, much less seen; and because of this, the place was overrun with mice—they danced on the tables, made their nests in the featherbeds and ate whatever they pleased. All the people complained bitterly about this nuisance; even the King himself did—for since he had no way of keeping them out of his palace, they squeaked in every corner and gnawed at everything they could get their teeth into.

The boy took his cat to the palace where she went briskly to work. After several big rooms had been cleared of mice, the people, who had been breathlessly watching the chase, begged the King to buy this marvel on four legs for the good of the kingdom.

This the King was willing to do, and asked the boy what he wanted for his cat.

"A mule," said the boy, "with as much gold as it can carry."

" 'Tis well worth it," said the King, and so while the boy went home with his mule and his treasure, the cat made merry with the mice in the King's castle. She got rid of more mice than could be counted, but after a while, since this hot wild chase made her very warm and thirsty, she stood in the middle of the big room, lifted her head and cried, "Miau! Miau! Miau!"

Upon hearing these strange sounds, the King and his people were terrified, and ran out of the castle and into the courtyard where they stood around in anxious groups. The King, at a loss as to what should be done, called a meeting of his advisers and, after a long and solemn conference, it was decided that a special envoy should be sent to negotiate with the wild, fierce beast.

The envoy went—but not too near—and said, "His Majesty the King is no longer desirous of your presence, and wishes to know this: namely, must he use force or are you willing to leave the castle peacefully and of your own accord?"

The poor cat, now almost mad with thirst, could only cry, "May-ow, May-ow, May-ow!"

The envoy, however, thought the cat was saying, "Nay-oh, Nay-oh, Nay-oh!" so he went to the King and announced, "Your Majesty, the creature answers in the negative."

"Well then," said the King sternly, and his advisers nodded their heads in agreement, "if the monster will not leave of his own free will, he must be made to leave by force."

So they brought out their cannons and began shooting at the castle, which soon burst into flames. When the fire reached the King's chamber where the thirsty cat was still *miauing* at the top of her voice, she sprang out of the window and ran and ran to the island's edge where she could drink her fill of water, and then, with the boom of the cannons still ringing in her ears, she swam away to the mainland.

"There she goes, and a good thing too!" cried the people, and so, because of their ignorance, they were again at the mercy of the mice, and are so still for all I know.

THE SORCERER'S APPRENTICE

A MAN found himself in need of a helper for his work-shop, and one day as he was walking along the outskirts of a little hamlet he met a boy with a bundle slung over his shoulder. Stopping him, the man said, "Good morning, my lad. I am looking for an apprentice. Have you a master?"

"No," said the boy, "I have just this morning said good-bye to my mother and am now off to find myself a trade."

"Good," said the man. "You look as though you might be just the lad I need. But wait, do you know anything about reading and writing?"

"Oh yes!" said the boy.

"Too bad!" said the man. "You won't do after all. I have no use for anyone who can read and write."

"Pardon me?" said the boy. "If it was *reading* and *writing* you were talking about, I misunderstood you. I thought you asked if I knew anything about *eating* and *fighting*—those two things I am able to do well, but as to reading and writing that is · something I know nothing about."

"Well!" cried the man. "Then you are just the fellow I want. Come with me to my workshop, and I will show you what to do."

The boy, however, had had his wits about him. He could read and write well enough and had only pretended to be a fool. Wondering why a man should prefer to have an unschooled helper, he thought to himself, "I smell a rat. There is something strange about this, and I had better keep my eyes and ears open."

While he was pondering over this, his new master was leading him into the heart of a deep forest. Here in a small clearing stood a house and, as soon as they entered it, the boy could see that this was no ordinary workshop.

At one end of a big room was a huge hearth with a copper cauldron hanging in it; at the other end was a small alcove lined with many big books. A mortar and pestle stood on a bench; bottles and sieves, measuring scales and oddly-shaped glassware were strewn about on the table.

Well! It did not take the clever young apprentice very long to realize that he was working for a magician or sorcerer of some kind and so, although he pretended to be quite stupid, he kept his eyes and ears open, and tried to learn all he could.

"Sorcery—that is a trade I would dearly love to master!" said the boy to himself. "A mouthful of good chants and charms would never come amiss to a poor fellow like me, and with them I might even be able to do some good in the world."

There were many things the boy had to do. Sometimes he was ordered to stir the evil-smelling broths which bubbled in the big copper cauldron; at other times he had to grind up herbs and berries—and other things too gruesome to mention—in the big mortar and pestle. It was also his task to sweep up the workshop, to keep the fire burning in the big hearth, and to gather the strange materials needed by the man for the broths and brews he was always mixing.

This went on day after day, week after week, and month after month, until the boy was almost beside himself with curiosity. He was most curious about the thick heavy books in the alcove. How often he had wondered about them, and how many times had he been tempted to take a peep between their covers! But, remembering that he was not supposed to know how to read or write, he had been wise enough never to show the least interest in them. At last there came a day when he made up his mind to see what was in them, no matter what the risk.

"I'll try it before another day dawns," he thought.

That night he waited until the sorcerer was sound asleep and was snoring loudly in his bedchamber; then, creeping out of his straw couch, the boy took a light into the corner of the alcove and began paging through one of the heavy volumes. What was written in them has never been told, but they were conjuring books, each and every one of them; and from that time on, the boy read in them silently, secretly, for an hour or two, night after night. In this way he learned many magic tricks: chants and charms and countercharms; recipes for philters and potions, for broths and brews and witches' stews; signs mystic and cabalistic, and other helpful spells of many kinds. All these he memorized carefully, and

200

THE BOY BEGAN PAGING THROUGH ONE OF THE HEAVY VOLUMES

it was not long before he sometimes was able to figure
out what kind of charms his master was working, what
brand of potion he was mixing, what sort of stews he
was brewing. And what kind of charms and potions and
stews were they? Alas, they were all wicked ones! Now
the boy knew that he was not working for an ordinary
magician, but for a cruel, dangerous sorcerer. And
because of this, the boy made a plan, a bold one.

He went on with his nightly studies until his head
was swarming with magic recipes and incantations. He
even had time to work at them in the daytime, for the
sorcerer sometimes left the workshop for hours—working

harm and havoc on mortals, no doubt. At such times the boy would try out a few bits of his newly-learned wisdom. He began with simple things, such as changing the cat into a bee and back to cat again, making a viper out of the poker, an imp out of the broom, and so on. Sometimes he was successful, often he was not; so he said to himself, "The time is not yet ripe."

One day, after the sorcerer had again gone forth on one of his mysterious trips, the boy hurried through his work, and had just settled himself in the dingy alcove with one of the conjuring books on his knees, when the master returned unexpectedly. The boy, thinking fast, pointed smilingly at one of the pictures, after which he quietly closed the book and went on with his work as though nothing were amiss.

But the sorcerer was not deceived.

"If the wretch can read," he thought, "he may learn how to outwit me. And I can't send him off with a beating and a 'bad speed to you', either—doubtless he knows too much already and will reveal all my fine mean tricks, and then I can't have any more sport working mischief on man and beast."

He acted quickly.

With one leap he rushed at the boy, who in turn made a spring for the door.

"Stop!" cried the sorcerer. "You shall not escape me!"

He was about to grab the boy by the collar when the quick-witted lad mumbled a powerful incantation by which he changed himself into a bird—and—Wootsch!—he had flown into the woods.

The sorcerer, not to be outdone, shouted a charm, thus changing himself into a larger bird—and Whoosh!—he was after the little one.

With a new incantation the boy made himself into a fish—and Whish!—he was swimming across a big pond.

But the master was equal to this, for, with a few words he made himself into a fish too, a big one, and swam after the little one.

At this the boy changed himself into a still bigger fish but the magician, by a master stroke, turned himself into a tiny kernel of grain and rolled into a small crack in a stone where the fish couldn't touch him.

Quickly the boy changed himself into a rooster, and—Peck! Peck! Peck!—with his sharp beak he snapped at the kernel of grain and ate it up.

That was the end of the wicked sorcerer, and the boy

became the owner of the magic workshop. And wasn't it
fine that all the powers and ingredients which had been
used for evil by the sorcerer were now in the hands of a
boy who would use them only for the good of man and
beast?

IRON HANS

THERE was a King who had a large and beautiful forest in which roamed wild animals of many kinds. One day he sent a hunter into these woods to shoot him a deer. The hunter went, but when evening came he did not return.

"Perhaps an accident has befallen him," said the King, and the following day he sent two other hunters to search for the first, but they too did not return.

On the third day the King called out all his remaining hunters, saying, "Search the entire forest and do not stop until you have found the three lost ones." But of these none came back either, nor did the pack of hounds which had been taken along on the search. From that time on, no one dared venture into the forest, which now lay wrapped in deep silence from one year's end to another and showed no signs of life except for an occasional hawk or eagle soaring above its branches.

This lasted for many years, but one day a strange hunter with a dog presented himself to the King and offered to enter the forest in order to discover its mystery. The King hesitated, saying, "It is an uncanny and dangerous place. I fear it will go no better with you than with the rest. You will never return."

Said the hunter, "Your Majesty, I know nothing of fear. If you will but grant me permission, I will go at my own risk."

Reluctantly the King consented and the hunter, taking his dog, entered the deep silent forest. It was not long before his dog, with sharp, excited barks, was following a scent; but after running a few steps, he stopped short on the bank of a deep pool, barking wildly. The next moment a large naked arm rose out of the pool, seized the dog and pulled him into the water. Seeing this, the hunter hurried back to the castle and fetched three men with buckets with which they began to scoop the water out of the pool.

They dipped and dipped until the pool was empty, but there in its muddy bottom was no dog, only a huge, wild-looking man. His powerful body was brown like rusted iron; his long tangled hair, rusty-red too, straggled over his face and hung down to his knees. Quickly the hunter and his three helpers leaped upon the wild man, bound him with cords and led him to the King's castle.

The King had the huge, silent creature put into an iron cage in the courtyard, forbidding anyone to release him on pain of death. To make sure of this, he had the door fitted with a big strong lock, the key of which he gave to the Queen for safekeeping. People came from far and near to look at the hunter's strange catch, marveled at the red-brown monster and, because he was the color of rusted iron and looked so strong besides, they called him Iron Hans.

After this anyone could again enter the forest with safety.

.   .   .   .   .

The King had a little blond-haired son eight years old, and his name was Prince Harald. The little boy played often in the courtyard, and one day as he was tossing his golden ball into the air it fell within the iron cage.

Harald ran to the cage and said, "Iron Hans, give me back my ball."

"No," said the man, "you shall not have it unless you open the door of my cage and let me out."

"Oh no, I can't do that," said the boy. "My papa has forbidden it," and ran away.

The next day Harald came back and again asked for his ball, but Iron Hans said, "Open my door and you shall have it."

"No, I can't do that," said Harald, and ran away as before.

By the third day the little boy wanted his ball so much that he didn't run away. "You may as well give me my ball," he said to Iron Hans, "for even if I wanted to open the door, I couldn't do it. The key is hidden away."

"Oh, as to that," said the man, "the key lies under your mother's pillow. You could easily get it."

As chance would have it, the King was off on a hunting trip that day, and since Harald knew that his mother was not in her room, he got the key, hurried back to the cage and unlocked it. The iron door was heavy and as it swung open the little Prince pinched his finger in it. Iron Hans tossed him the ball, dashed out of the cage and fled toward the forest.

But now Harald was worried over what he had done and called out after the running man, "Oh wild man! Iron Hans! Don't run away or I'll surely get a spanking."

At this, Iron Hans turned around and came back. Then, lifting the little Prince upon his wide shoulders, he strode off with him into the forest.

When the King returned from his hunting trip and saw the empty cage, he asked the Queen how this had come to pass. She had noticed nothing, and when she looked for the key and found it gone, she became alarmed and called her little son, but there was no answer. Now

the King and Queen could guess what had happened. They sent many people to search for the missing Prince but as no one found him, heavy mourning fell over the castle and over all the land.

.   .   .   .   .

In the meantime Iron Hans had walked steadily on until he had reached the middle of the forest where he lived. Then, lifting little Harald from his shoulders, he said kindly, "You freed me, little Prince. I am grateful to you and I won't hurt you. If you do as I say, you will have it easy enough here with me. I have much hidden treasure and more gold than anyone can guess." Then he made a soft bed of moss for the boy who soon fell fast asleep.

The next morning Iron Hans led him to a well.

"Look," he said, "this is a golden well and in order that it may stay pure and clear it must be watched so that it won't be spoiled. Every day while I am gone you must sit here and see that nothing falls into the water. In the evening I will come and see if you have obeyed my order."

Little Harald sat at the edge of the golden well and

found it amusing to watch the pretty creatures which lived in it. Glittering fish darted here and there, golden frogs leaped and splashed about, gilded bugs and eels wriggled in and out among the ripples. For hours he gazed, being careful to let nothing fall into the water, but suddenly his finger, which had been pinched in the cage door the day before, began to ache so much that, before he knew what he was doing, he had dipped it into the cool water to ease the pain. He pulled it out again very quickly but it was too late—the finger had become all gilded, and no matter how hard he rubbed it, the gold would not come off.

That evening when Iron Hans returned, he said, "What has happened to my well?"

"Nothing, nothing," said the poor boy, trying to hide his finger behind his back.

But Iron Hans said, "I know. You have dipped your finger into the water. We'll let it pass this time, but take care that it doesn't happen again."

Early the next morning after Iron Hans had gone away, Harald sat watching the well once more. His finger was still aching and once, as a twinge of pain went through it, he jerked up his hand which, as ill luck

213

would have it, brushed a hair loose from his head. The hair fell into the well and although Harald snatched it out immediately, it was already coated with gold.

When Iron Hans returned that evening he knew at once what had happened. "You have let one of your hairs fall into the water," he said. "At this rate my golden well will soon be spoiled. I'll overlook it just once more, but if anything else falls into the well it will be completely spoiled, so I must warn you to be more careful."

On the third day Harald sat at the well and took care not to move his finger, no matter how much it pained him. There he sat and watched, waiting for evening to come. He became so weary of doing nothing that when he saw his reflection in the golden water mirror, he bent over to get a good look at himself. So interested did he become in this that he bent farther and farther over the well until, Whish! the ends of his long wavy hair slid down over his shoulders and dropped into the water. Quickly he raised himself up, but all of his hair was already gilded and shone like the sun. Full of alarm, he took his kerchief, and cramming his golden curls under it, wrapped it carefully and tightly about his head so that not a single strand of hair was visible.

When Iron Hans came home he looked very stern. "Take off your kerchief!" he said.

Harald had to obey, and as he did so, his hair tumbled in golden waves about his shoulders, and although he begged to be given another chance, Iron Hans remained firm.

"No," said he. "You have not stood the trial and have spoiled my well, so I can't keep you here any longer. You must go out into the world where—prince or no prince—you must shift for yourself and get along as best you can. But I know you did not mean to do wrong, so I will always be your friend. If you are ever in trouble, come to my forest and call me. Then I will come out and help you."

.　　.　　.　　.　　.

Harald left the forest and walked over trodden and untrodden paths until at length he reached a great city. There he asked for work, but since a prince is not taught to earn his living there was nothing he could do and no one had any need for him. Yet, because he was a courteous and winsome lad, the people felt sorry for him and said, "Go to the King's palace. They need many servants there, and perhaps a light task could be found for a genteel boy like you."

At the palace there seemed to be no place for him either, but at last the servants, charmed by his pleasant manner, found a place for him as gardener's helper. And now, in good weather and bad, Harald toiled away at his new task. All day long he hoed and raked, planted seeds and pulled weeds, and carried pails of water for the flowers and vegetables. Always he wore a hat to hide his gilded hair, but one hot day in summer as he was working alone in the garden, he became so warm that he had to remove his hat for a few minutes in order to cool his head. As the sun shone on his tresses, they gleamed so brightly that their golden beams were reflected on the walls of one of the castle chambers which, as luck would have it, belonged to the King's young daughter. Looking out of the window to see what caused these glancing beams, the girl beheld Harald with his gleaming locks, working busily in the garden.

"Such wondrous hair!" she thought. "I would like to get a better look at it," and so, stretching her head out of the window, she called, "Oh, garden boy! Bring me a bouquet of flowers."

Hurriedly Harald clapped his hat on his head, stuffed the clusters of golden curls under its crown, plucked a handful of flowers and carried them to the young Princess. But she was deeply disappointed at seeing his hair hidden away, and said, "Is that a way—to keep on your hat in the presence of a princess?"

"I daren't take it off," said the boy with downcast eyes. "My head is too dirty."

But the Princess did not believe him. She made a quick grab at his hat and pulled it off, and out burst his gilded curls tumbling wave upon wave over his shoulders. The boy, although miserable, looked so charming in his confusion that the Princess, entranced, asked him for more flowers the next day.

He had to obey, of course, and when he brought her the bouquet, she again made a grab for his hat, but this time he was able to keep his curls covered by clutching the hat with his hands.

On the third day things went no better for the Princess, for again the boy outwitted her. Rushing into her room, he thrust the flowers into her hand and ducked out of the door before she could reach for his hat.

．　　．　　．　　．　　．

Time flowed on and there came a day when there was dire trouble in the land. An invading army was at the country's borders, and the worried King gathered his warriors together to defend his people against the foe, which was wild and ruthless and very strong.

As the village folk were standing about in groups watching the mustering of the troops, Harald, who was among them, said, "I'm getting to be a big boy now, and if someone will give me a horse, I'll go out and help save our country."

All the folk laughed and said to each other, "Did you ever hear the like? That garden boy! What can he do anyway?" And the soldiers, who were laughing louder than all the rest, turned to him and said, "We're off to battle with our horses, but after we're gone, look around in the stable. We'll leave a steed for you—see what you can do with it!"

After they had galloped away on their fine strong horses, Harald went into the stable and dragged out the only horse that was left. A broken-down nag it was— a pitiful, bony creature which was lame in one foot; and as it limped along, its hoofs went:

> Hickelty, hickelty
> Hickelty, hunkipuss
> Hickelty, hickelty
> Hickelty, hunk!

Yes, it was a sorry steed, indeed, that the soldiers had left behind, but Harald, nothing daunted, leaped on the miserable creature's back and, with the old men, women and children shouting and jeering at what they considered the drollest sight they had ever seen, rode calmly away.

But he did not ride to the battle on his three-legged nag, oh no! He stayed on the road only as long as he was within sight of the mocking mob, then he turned off and rode to the edge of his old friend's forest.

"Iron Hans! Iron Hans! Iron Hans!" he called, so loudly that it echoed through the trees.

In a trice Iron Hans appeared, big and brown as ever, saying, "Well, how are you, my boy, and what can I do for you?"

"I would like to help defend our country against the wild and ruthless foe," said Harald, "and for this I need a good strong steed."

"That you shall have," said Iron Hans. "That, and more besides."

He vanished into the depths of the forest and before long a groom appeared, carrying a suit of armor and leading a spirited charger which was snorting and champing, and stamping proudly with its hoofs. The groom offered Harald the horse, also the suit of armor, complete with helmet, shield and spear. After handing his poor

220

old nag over to the groom, our gardener Prince donned the shining armor, grasped his shield and spear and then, leaping on his fiery charger, he took the reins and started to gallop away. As he did so, he heard a loud clanking of iron armor and a clatter of shields and spears behind him, and when he turned around he saw a solid mass of mounted cavalry, all clad in iron, following him. It was his army and he was their general!

Off went Harald and his Iron Host, charging into the thickest of the fray. Such a gallant army it was, and such a valiant leader was our Harald, that the cruel invading horde was soon routed and fleeing like leaves before a stormy gale.

Great cheers rose from the King's people but, not knowing who the strange general was, they waited for him to return and present himself to the King. Prince Harald did not do so. Instead, leading his Iron Host through secret ways back to the forest, he called Iron Hans and said, "Here, dear friend, take back your steed and armor, and this gallant army too—and give me, please, my humble gardener's clothes and my poor old three-legged horse."

Iron Hans did so; and Harald hobbled back toward

the castle on his lame nag, whose hoofs, clattering on the cobblestones, went:

Hickelty, hickelty
Hickelty, hunkipuss
Hickelty, hickelty,
Hickelty, hunk!

As he approached the town he was greeted by scoffs and jeers as before. "Oh ho! Oho!" cried the people. "Here comes our Hickelty Hunkipuss back again." And when they asked him sneeringly behind what hedges he had lain asleep during the battle, he said quietly, "I did the best I could and it would have gone badly without me."

At this the people screamed with laughter and said, "Our brave Hunkipuss, what a warrior he is!"

The King meantime had returned from the battlefield full of joy over the outcome of the battle, but when his Princess daughter told him how glad she was that he had won, he said, "It was not I who won the battle, child. The foe was cruel and bold, and outnumbered us by hundreds. We were getting the worst of it when there came a strange knight with a mighty iron-clad army of his own, and before anyone could tell what was happening, he had routed the enemy."

The Princess was interested. "Who was the knight?" she asked. "And where is he now?"

"Ah, that I don't know!" said her father. "For he rode after the fleeing enemy and never came back."

. . . . . .

The next day the King, who was determined to find out who had saved his country from the invaders, said, "Daughter, I have a plan. I will give a grand three-day festival to celebrate our victory. Every day you will stand on your balcony and toss a golden apple among the multitude. This will draw all kinds of people from far and near—perhaps our mysterious knight will come too." At this the Princess clapped her hands joyfully for she too was full of curiosity over this strangely modest knight.

The King was right. People flocked to the big Victory Festival, and Harald, when he heard of it, hurried to the edge of the big forest and called his old friend Iron Hans.

"What is your wish, my boy?" asked Iron Hans when he appeared.

Harald answered, "The King's beautiful daughter will toss out a golden ball at the big Victory Festival. I should like to be the one to catch it."

"It is as good as done, my lad," said Iron Hans, "and aside from that you shall have a suit of scarlet armor and a proud chestnut bay to ride upon."

And so it happened that on the first day of the festival Harald, dressed in a suit of flashing scarlet armor, and with his golden locks hidden away under a plumed helmet of the same color, came cantering along on a beautiful chestnut bay and placed himself among the knights. No one knew him. When the Princess stepped out upon her balcony and tossed the golden apple among the multitude, it was the knight in scarlet armor who caught it; but as soon as his fingers closed over the apple, he galloped away.

On the second day Iron Hans provided Harald with

a different outfit, so that this time he appeared as a white knight, riding on a milk-white charger. Again he caught the golden apple and galloped away before anyone knew what was happening.

The King did not like this. "That is not allowed!" he said angrily. "He must appear before me and disclose his name!" Then, calling his guards, he said, "Tomorrow if the strange knight gallops away as before, pursue and capture him, and bring him to me."

On the third day Iron Hans gave Harald a suit of lustrous black armor and a glossy black steed to ride upon. Again he caught the golden apple before anyone else could do so, but this time the King's guards gave him hot pursuit as he galloped away. One of these came so close to him that he pierced Harald's armor and pricked his leg with the tip of his sword, so that Harold had to ride furiously to escape him. He got away but his horse galloped so fast that his helmet flew from his head, and as his golden locks burst out and rolled over his shoulders, gleaming and glittering in the sunlight, the people who were watching could see that he had golden hair.

To the young Princess those golden locks seemed

strangely familiar, and the next day she paid the gardener a visit. "And how is your garden-boy getting along these days?" she asked him.

"Oh that boy!" chuckled the gardener. "Not long ago he tried to go to battle on an old three-legged nag. We call him Hickelty Hunkipuss now."

"And these last three days," continued the Princess, "has he been working all the time?"

"Oh no," said the gardener. "Every day he asked me to let him off to watch the festival, and last night when he returned, he showed my children three golden apples. That lad, I can't make him out!"

When the Princess hurried to her father and told him all she knew, he acted at once.

"The garden-boy is to appear before me immediately," was his command, and Harald obeyed promptly but with his hat on as usual. At this the King frowned with displeasure. "Don't you even know enough to remove your hat in the presence of a king?" he thundered out.

Meekly Harald said, "Oh Your Majesty, I cannot. My head is too dirty." He bowed low, and as he did so, the Princess reached out and swiftly snatched off his hat. Out rolled the golden glory of his hair, wave upon wave over his young shoulders, and was so beautiful that all the court, even the King, were amazed at the dazzling sight.

"Ah!" said the King. "So you are the knight who came every day in a different color of armor and caught the golden apple!"

"I cannot deny it, Your Majesty," said Harald. He took the three golden apples out of his pocket, handed them to the King, and added, "If you desire further proof of it, here is the wound in my leg, given to me by one of your men only yesterday. And I am that other knight too—the mysterious general who came with a big iron-clad army to fight for you."

"My boy," said the King. "I see you are not an ordinary garden boy. Who is your father?"

"A king," said Harald.

"And what can I do to show you my gratitude and esteem?" asked the King.

"You might give me your daughter for my future bride," said Harald.

The Princess laughed and clapped her hands.

"As soon as I saw his golden hair," she said, "I knew he was something out of the ordinary!"

She ran over and kissed him, and it was not long before they celebrated their wedding.

As they all sat at the wedding feast, full of joy and gaiety, the music suddenly ceased, the door opened slowly, and a proud king, followed by an imposing retinue, strode in. Approaching Harald, he said, "I am your old friend, Iron Hans. I was bewitched into a wild man and you freed me. I have a mighty kingdom and no son of my own. All my treasures and riches shall be yours."

Harald was overjoyed but suddenly his face clouded as he said, "But all the people who were lost in the big forest—where are they?"

"They were all freed with me and have returned to their homes," said Iron Hans. "Yes, even the little dog which belonged to the brave hunter who caught me and released me from the pool."

"And my father and mother," asked Harald, "are they alive and well?"

"They are," said Iron Hans, "and are coming to your wedding. They are on their way—no, they are here!"

I will leave you to guess whether this was a happy wedding festival or not!

JORINDA AND JORINGEL

I DON'T know if it is still there, but at one time there was an old grey castle in the middle of a deep, dense forest where lived an old woman who was a witch. By day she took the form of an owl or a cat, but after sundown she always became a human being again. She had many cruel tricks but the one she liked best was her Magic Circle Enchantment, for with this she could catch anyone who came within a hundred steps of the grey wall surrounding her castle.

If it was a man or boy who strayed beyond this danger line, he became rooted to the ground and could neither move nor talk until the Old One chose to disenchant him. If it was a young girl who stepped within the Magic

Circle, the old enchantress turned her into a bird, packed her into a covered basket and carried her into a great hall inside her castle. And you can see how great was her wickedness when I tell you that in her home she already had seven thousand such baskets, each containing a captive bird which had once been a maiden.

Now it happened that in this forest, and not far from the witch's domain, there lived two young friends who loved each other dearly. One was a girl and her name was Jorinda. The other, a boy, was called Joringel.

One balmy summer evening these two set out for a stroll in the woods. Hand in hand they went, as was their wont, and all about them everything was calm and beautiful. The birds twittered and fluttered among the leaves. The sunbeams slanted between the tree trunks and fell in shining ribbons against the dark green of the forest. The two children were peaceful and happy.

"How beautiful it is!" said Joringel. "But we must be careful not to wander into the witch's Magic Circle."

"Oh, we can't be near it yet," said Jorinda light-heartedly; and so they walked on, watching the rabbits and squirrels, picking a flower here and there.

But before long their happy mood dwindled away. The

leaves began to rustle mournfully, the birds became
quieter and quieter. Jorinda and Joringel, they knew not
why, grew silent and solemn. On and on they walked,
slowly now, and with heavy steps. A turtle dove was
singing its song among the beeches, and the children

became strangely sad. Tears rolled down Jorinda's cheeks; Joringel was filled with a nameless woe. Confused and forlorn, they looked for the way home but could not find it.

"Oh, I think we are lost!" said Joringel, and Jorinda knew he was right.

The sun was sinking fast. One half of its glowing face still showed above the rim of a distant mountain top, the other half had already dropped out of sight. Joringel, searching for a path, spied something grey showing between the twigs of a tall thicket and became alarmed, for he knew this could be only one thing: the grey stone wall of the witch's domain. Jorinda seemed to notice nothing and was acting strangely. In the fading light she had sunk down on the grass and now she was singing, almost sobbing:

> My birdie with the red, red ring
> Cries sorrow, sorrow, sorrow.
> It sings the end of everything.
> Oh sorrow, sorrow, sor — tsick-eet!
> tsick-eet!
> tsick-eet!

Joringel turned quickly and looked at Jorinda. In the midst of her song she had changed into a singing nightingale with a beautiful red ring around her throat; and now an owl with glowing eyes and a sharp, hooked beak was flying over them.

Three times the owl circled over them, and three times she screeched, "Shoo hoo! hoo! hoo!"

Joringel could not move; he stood there motionless as a stone—could not walk, could not weep, could not talk. The sun sank behind the mountain top—then it was gone. The owl disappeared behind a thicket, and in the next moment out came a bent old woman carrying a covered wicker basket. Yellow and haggard she was, with big red owlish eyes and a beak-like nose which almost touched her chin. Muttering to herself, she caught the little nightingale who had once been Jorinda, clapped the bird into her basket and hobbled off toward the old grey castle, cackling happily.

As her footsteps rustled off among the leaves, darkness closed in dusky folds over the forest, and Joringel, standing speechless and motionless as before, was left alone. But although he could not speak, he was still able to think well enough, and what he thought was: "That was the old witch, and she has taken my dear little Jorinda into her grey castle forever!"

Before long the Old One returned and, standing before Joringel, chanted in a hollow voice:

Greetings, Zachiel, now to thee!
When the little moonbeams fall
On the basket in my hall,
Loose this lad and set him free.

When Joringel heard these strange words he was puzzled. He did not know who this Zachiel might be, but he soon guessed the meaning of the rest of the song, for suddenly, as the moon stole out from behind a cloud, he found he could move and talk once more. Knowing himself to be freed, he now wished to free Jorinda also, so he fell on his knees before the old sorceress and begged her to release his playmate.

But the Old One said, "You'll never get her back."

Joringel pleaded and prayed and sobbed—it was all in vain. With a triumphant cackle the Old One turned her back on him, hobbled away, and soon was out of sight and hearing.

"Oh, what will become of me now?" moaned the boy. He made his way out of the forest and, dazed with sorrow, wandered off until he came to a strange village. Here he hired himself out as a shepherd and herded sheep for many a long month.

At last, one night, he had a dream. He dreamt he found a red, red flower, in the heart of which lay a wondrous pearl. Plucking the flower, he walked without fear to the grey castle where all that he touched with the flower became disenchanted, and in this way he freed his dear Jorinda. That was his dream.

When he awoke the next morning, he set out to search for such a magic flower. Up the steep mountains he went, through villages and valleys, and into the depths of tangled woodlands. For eight days he wandered thus, and on the morning of the ninth day he found a red, red flower! In its rosy blossom-cup nestled a morning dewdrop, laughing and sparkling and more beautiful than a pearl. Carefully he plucked the flower and carefully he held it too, as he walked day and night until he reached the witch's forest.

When he came within a hundred paces of the witch's domain he did not become rooted to the ground as before. Instead, he walked to the ponderous gate and touched it with his red, red flower. The gate sprang open and Joringel walked into the courtyard, listening for the sound of the birds. Yes, he could hear something—a thousand-throated twittering and trilling and warbling.

But where were the birds? Where in that big castle was the great hall in which the Old One kept the seven thousand enchanted maidens and his dear Jorinda-nightingale? Entering the castle on tiptoe, Joringel made his way toward the warbling sounds, and at last, after winding his way through a maze of chambers and corridors, he came upon a large hall from which issued the music and fluttering of myriads of birds.

The door of the room was ajar and Joringel peered in. What a sight he beheld! On the floor, on the walls, on the shelves and tables and chairs and benches, were seven thousand birds in seven thousand baskets; and there, too, was the old sorceress busily feeding her flock of songsters. As Joringel paused at the door, wondering what to do next, the Old One looked up. When she saw him her face twisted up in fury and then, spitting poison and gall with each step, she advanced threateningly toward him. But Joringel was not to be frightened so easily. Quickly he held out his red, red flower, and as he did so the old sorceress was forced to stop; and when she found she could not get within two steps of him, she fumed and screamed and scolded.

Joringel took no notice of her. He had other things

to do, and his only thought was for his beloved Jorinda. She was somewhere in the room; he must find her and free her. From basket to basket he went, peeping into every one of them in search of his nightingale. But just as there were hundreds of canaries, hundreds of song sparrows, hundreds of wrens, thrushes, swallows and linnets in the baskets, so there were hundreds of night-ingales, too. How would he ever be able to tell which one of these was Jorinda? While he was searching, he kept an eye on the Old One too, and suddenly, out of the corner of his eyes, he saw that she was up to some mischief. She had ceased scolding and screeching, had stealthily picked up one of the baskets, and was now trying to sneak off with it toward another door.

"That looks queer!" thought Joringel and acted quickly. Leaping in front of her, he touched first the cage, then the witch, with his red, red flower. As he did so, the Old One lost all spirit and stood defeated and limp before him, for now she was powerless and could never enchant him or anyone else again. In her hand she held an empty basket, and in front of him stood Jorinda, a nightingale no longer, but a girl with happy dancing eyes and arms outstretched in welcome.

"Oh Jorinda!" cried the boy. "Now we can go home and be happy together as before. But wait! I have a pleasant task to do before we leave," and, going all around the room from basket to basket, he touched each one with his magic flower. And—oh wonder and joy!— as he did so, one bird after another stopped singing, the lid of each basket popped open, and out of every one sprang a happy, grateful maiden.

Yes, now all of the seven thousand baskets were empty,

and seven thousand lovely maidens crowded the great hall, curtsying and thanking Joringel for freeing them. And then, leaving the old sorceress alone and powerless in her big gloomy castle, the maidens returned to their homes and lived happily ever after; and Jorinda and Joringel did the same.

THE WOLF AND THE
SEVEN LITTLE KIDS

ONCE there was a mother goat—her name was
Mother Nanny. She had seven little baby goats which,
as you know, are called kids, and these she loved as
dearly as any other mother loves her children.

One day Mother Nanny wanted to go into the woods
to get some food, so she called her seven little kids and
said, "Children dear, I am going away to get you
something to eat. Bolt the door after me when I leave,

and watch out for the wolf—that wolf, he would like nothing better than to get in here and eat you up. He's a wicked wolf, and such a wise one that he often pretends to be someone else. But remember, my dears, you can always know him by two things: his loud harsh voice and his rough black paws."

The seven little kids listened carefully to their mother's words, then said, "Don't worry, Mother Nanny—we'll be careful." Then the mother goat gave a few affectionate bleats and went on her way.

The seven little kids bolted the door and began playing, but it was not long before there was a loud knock on the door. Then a loud harsh voice shouted:

"OPEN THE DOOR, MY SWEET LITTLE CHILDREN. HERE IS YOUR MOTHER AND SHE HAS BROUGHT A DAINTY MORSEL FOR EACH OF YOU."

But the seven little kids knew better, and they said, "No! We won't open the door. You are not our mother. She has a soft gentle voice, but yours is harsh and loud. *You* are the wolf!"

THE WOLF AND THE SEVEN LITTLE KIDS

The wolf slunk away and went to a store where he bought a big lump of chalk which he ate in order to make his voice soft and fine. Then he trotted softly back to the home of the seven little kids and said sweetly:

> "Open the door, my little darlings.
> Here is your Nanny-mother, back from
> the woods with a luscious tid-bit for
> each of you."

This time the little kids thought it really was their mother, but just as they were about to pull back the bolt, they caught a glimpse of the wolf's shaggy black paw resting against the window sill. So they cried, "No! We won't open the door. You are not our mother. She has a soft white paw and yours is rough and black. *You* are the wolf!"

Away went the wolf again, this time to the baker's shop.

"I have hurt my foot," he said to the baker. "Spread some dough over it."

When the baker had done this the wolf ran to the miller, held up his doughy paw and said, "Miller, I have hurt my foot. Sprinkle it well with white flour."

The miller, who was afraid the wolf might be up to

some mischief, said bravely, "What do you mean? A little dough and flour won't heal your foot."

"Do as I tell you!" snarled the wolf, "or I'll eat you up!"

This frightened the miller. He did as he was told. And the wolf, carefully holding up his floury paw, went for the third time to the home of the seven little kids. He knocked softly on the door and said in gentle tones:

"Open the door, my little darlings.
Your own dear mother has come back
at last and has brought something
good from the forest for each of you."

The mouths of the seven little kids watered, but still they were careful and said, "First show us your paw."

The wolf placed his floury paw on the edge of the window sill, and when the seven little kids saw how soft and white it was, they looked at each other and said, "Such a sweet gentle voice and such a soft white paw— it *must* be our Nanny-mother."

They drew back the bolt and opened the door, and who came in? The wicked, wicked wolf came in and started running after them.

The seven little kids were terrified and scurried in all directions, trying to hide themselves.

One sprang under the table.

The second into the bed.

The third into the oven.

The fourth into the kitchen.

The fifth into the cupboard.

The sixth beneath the wash-bowl.

The seventh and smallest scrambled into the big grandfather's clock in the corner.

But the wolf ran after them and, one after the other, he found the poor little kids and quickly swallowed them. That is, all but the youngest who had hidden in the grandfather's clock in the corner—the wolf didn't find him!

After his hearty meal the wolf felt too full and heavy and drowsy to go back to his home. He wobbled out of the door, laid himself down under a shade tree in the meadow, and fell into a heavy sleep.

When Mother Nanny returned from the woods, oh, what a sight met her eyes! The door was open, the house was topsy-turvy. Cupboards were agape, tables and chairs and benches were upset. The wash-bowl lay broken to bits, covers were ripped, pillows slashed, feathers were

lying and flying about. But where were her seven little
children?

Searching in every room and corner, she called each
of them by name—the first, the second, the third, the
fourth and fifth and sixth. There was no answer. But
when she called the seventh, she heard a tiny voice
calling, "Here I am, Mother Nanny. Here I am, shut
up in the grandfather's clock in the corner."

Mother Nanny opened the door of the clock and out
popped her baby, safe and sound but with sorrowful
news for the mother. Quickly the little goat told how

the wolf had come, how he had fooled them all first, then swallowed his six brothers and sisters—and now you can imagine how the mother wept over her poor children! At last, in her grief, she went outside and wandered off, she hardly knew why or where, and her little baby with her. When they reached the shade tree in the meadow, they saw the wicked wolf lying there all stuffed and puffed up, and snoring so hard that the earth shook beneath him and the treetops trembled above.

Mother Nanny and the baby kid walked around the sleeping wolf, and as they looked, something seemed to be squirming and wriggling in the puffed-up paunch of the wolf.

"Oh, heavens!" cried the Mother Goat. "Is it possible that my six little children are still alive in there?"

Quickly she sent the baby kid to fetch her sewing box, then whisked out her scissors, and with little snips and clips, carefully slit the wolf's puffy paunch. And then—

Out popped one.

No, out popped two.

No, three—no, four—no, five!

Oh, out popped six—

All six of the swallowed little kids!

That was a joy! They were as fresh and hearty as one could wish, for the greedy wolf had gulped them down whole and they were not hurt in the least. They were all so happy they began jumping around like a tailor at his wedding, until their mother said, "Come, come, we have no time to lose. Go and gather as many rocks as you can carry. We must stuff that wolf up again while he is still sound asleep, or he will guess what has happened."

The little kids brought rocks and stones and stuffed them into the wicked old creature until there was not room for a pebble more, after which Mother Nanny sewed him up so swiftly and neatly that he did not even stop snoring. Then she and her seven children hurried home and looked out of the window to see what would happen.

. . . . .

When the wolf awoke at last from his deep heavy sleep, he felt strange inside and very thirsty. He dragged himself up on all fours and started for the well, and as he hobbled and wobbled along with the rocks rattling in his paunch, he said to himself:

What rumbles and tumbles
Against my poor bones?
I thought they were kids
But I fear they are stones.

As he reached the well he bent down to lap up some water, but the weight of the rocks inside of him dragged him over the edge, and with a splash and a gurgle, he was gone and was never seen again.

Now the seven little kids, feeling safe and happy at last, ran outdoors and capered joyfully around the well, shouting, "The wolf is dead! The wolf is dead!" And so, with the wicked wolf out of the way, they and their mother lived happily ever after.

THE SHOEMAKER
AND THE ELVES

THERE was once a shoemaker who made shoes and
made them well. Yet luck was against him for, although
he worked hard every day, he became poorer and poorer
until he had nothing left but enough leather for one
pair of shoes.

That evening he cut out the leather for the last pair
of shoes, and then after laying the pieces in a neat row
on his workbench, he said his prayers and went peacefully to bed.

"I'll get up early in the morning," he thought. "Then
I can finish the shoes and perhaps sell them."

But when he arose the next morning, the pieces of cut
leather were nowhere to be seen, and in their stead
stood a pair of beautiful shoes, all finished to the last

251

seam, and sewn so neatly, too, that there was not a flaw nor a false stitch in them. The shoemaker was amazed and did not know what to make of it, but he picked up the shoes and set them out for sale. Soon a man came

and bought them, and because he was so pleased with their fine workmanship, he paid more than the usual price for them. With this money the shoemaker was able to buy enough leather for two pairs of shoes.

As before, he cut the leather for the next day's sewing, laid it out on his workbench and went to bed. In the morning, there again were the shoes—two pairs this time—all ready to wear. The hammer, the knife, the awl, the wax and twine, the needles and pegs, still lay about on the bench as though someone had been working there, yet no one could be seen. The shoemaker didn't know how such a thing could happen but he was glad it happened, all the same. Again he was lucky enough to sell the shoes for more than the usual price, and this time he was able to buy enough leather for four pairs of shoes.

Well, so it went on. Night after night he cut out the leather and laid it on his workbench; morning after morning, there stood a row of handsome shoes, ready to sell, ready to wear. And day after day buyers came and

paid such a good price for the shoes that the shoemaker was able to buy more and more leather, and sell more and more shoes until at last he was poor no longer and even became a well-to-do man.

Then one evening—it was not long before Christmas— the shoemaker, after laying out the leather for many pairs of shoes, went to his wife and said, "How would it be now, if we stayed awake tonight and watched for a while? I would like to see who it is, or what it can be, that is so good to us."

"Yes," said his wife, "that I would like to know too."

They lit a candle and set it on the table, then hid in a corner behind some clothes which were hanging there. Here they waited until at last, just at midnight, there came two pretty little elves without a stitch of clothing to cover them. Quickly the little creatures sprang upon the workbench and began making shoes. Swiftly and nimbly they worked—piercing and punching and sewing, pegging and pounding away with such skill that the man and his wife could scarcely believe their eyes.

And so the little elves worked on with tiny flying fingers, and didn't stop for a moment until all the shoes were finished down to the last stitch and peg. Then, in a twinkling, they leaped up and ran away. Next morning the woman said, "Husband, what I was going to say, those little elves have made us so rich—to show our thanks would be no more than right. There they run around, poor little wights, all bare and must surely freeze. Do you know what? I will make them some clothes and knit them each a pair of stockings. You can make them each a pair of little shoes, yes?"

Oh yes, the shoemaker would gladly do that. And so one evening, when everything was ready, they laid out their presents instead of the cut-out leather, then hid once more behind the clothes in the corner and waited to see what the little creatures would do.

At midnight, there came the two little elves, skipping along, ready to sit down and work as usual. They looked,

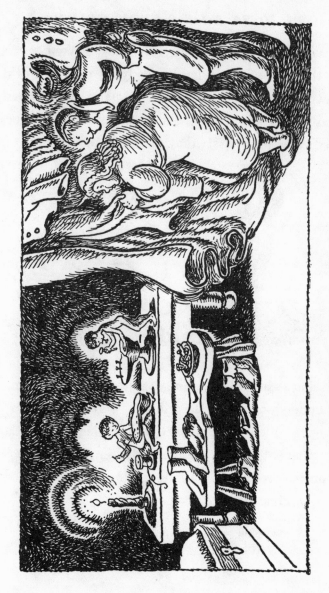

QUICKLY THE LITTLE CREATURES SPRANG UPON THE WORKBENCH

but saw no leather anywhere. They looked again and spied the row of little garments lying on the workbench: two little shirts and jerkins, two pairs of breeches, two peaked hats, four little stockings and four tiny shoes with pointed toes. At first they seemed puzzled, as though

wondering what these things were for, but then, when they understood that the clothes were meant for them, they were filled with joy. Quickly they picked up one little garment after another, dressing themselves with lightning speed; and all the time they laughed with delight, and sang:

> Now we are jaunty gentlemen,
> Why should we ever work again?

When they were fully dressed, from peaky hats to pointy toes, they began to skip and run around like wild, so glad and gleeful were they. There seemed to be no end to their capers as they leaped over the chairs, and delved among the shelves and benches, but at last, after spinning round and round like tiny tops, they clasped hands and went dancing out of the door.

They never came back, but the shoemaker and his wife were always lucky after that, and they never forgot the two little elves who had helped them in their time of need.

THE END